The Madness of May

Meredith Nicholson

Contents

THE MADNESS OF MAY

BY

Meredith Nicholson

I

Billy Deering let himself into his father's house near Radford Hills, Westchester County, and with a nod to Briggs, who came into the hall to take his hat and coat, began turning over the letters that lay on the table.

"Mr. Hood has arrived, sir," the servant announced. "I put him in the south guest-room."

Deering lifted his head with a jerk. "Hood--what Hood?"

"Mr. Hood is all I know, sir. He said he was expected--you had asked him for the night. If there's a mistake----"

Deering reached for his hat and coat, which Briggs still held. His face whitened, and the outstretched hand shook visibly. Briggs eyed him with grave concern, then took a step toward the stairway.

"If you wish, sir----"

"Never mind, Briggs," Deering snapped. "It's all right. I'd forgotten I had a guest coming; that's all."

He opened a letter with assumed carelessness and held it before his eyes until the door closed upon Briggs. Then his jaws tightened. He struck his hands together and mounted the steps doggedly, as though prepared for a disagreeable encounter.

All the way out on the train he had feared that this might happen. The long arm of the law was already clutching at his collar, but he had not reckoned with this quick retribution. The presence of the unknown man in the house could be explained on no other hypothesis than the discovery of his theft of two hundred thousand dollars in gilt-edged bonds from the banking-house of Deering, Gaylord & Co. It only remained for him to kill himself and escape from the shame that would follow exposure. He must do this at once, but first he would see who had been sent to apprehend him. Hood was an unfamiliar name; he had never known a

Hood anywhere, he was confident of that.

The house was ominously quiet. Deering paused when he reached his own room, glanced down the hall, then opened the door softly, and fell back with a gasp before the blaze of lights. There, lost in the recesses of a comfortable chair, with his legs thrown across the mahogany table, sat a man he had never seen before.

"Ah, Deering; very glad you've come," murmured the stranger, glancing up unhurriedly from his perusal of a newspaper.

He had evidently been reading for some time, as the floor was littered with papers. At this instant something in the page before him caught his attention and he deftly extracted a quarter of a column of text, pinched it with the scissors' points and dropped it on a pile of similar cuttings on the edge of the table.

"Just a moment!" he remarked in the tone of a man tolerant of interruptions, "and do pardon me for mussing up your room. I liked it better here than in the pink room your man gave me--no place there to put your legs! Creature of habit; can't rest without sticking my feet up."

He opened a fresh newspaper and ran his eyes over the first page with the trained glance of an expert exchange reader.

"The Minneapolis papers are usually worthless for my purposes, and yet occasionally they print something I wouldn't miss. I'm the best friend the 'buy your home paper' man has," he ran on musingly, skimming the page and ignoring Deering, who continued to stare in stupefied amazement from the doorway. "Ah!"

The scissors flashed and the unknown added another item to his collection.

"That's all," he remarked with a sigh. He dropped his feet to the floor, rose, and lazily stretched himself.

Tall, compactly built, a face weather-beaten where the flesh showed above a close-clipped brownish beard, and hair, slightly gray, brushed back smoothly from a broad forehead--these items Deering noted swiftly as he dragged himself across the threshold.

"Really, a day like this would put soul into a gargoyle," the stranger remarked, brushing the paper-shavings from his trousers. "Motored up from Jersey and had a grand time all the way. I walk, mostly, but commandeer a machine for long skips. To learn how to live, my dear boy, that's the great business! Not sure I've caught the trick, but I'm working at it, with such feeble talents as the gods have bestowed."

He filled a pipe deftly from a canvas bag, and drew the strings together with white, even teeth.

This cool, lounging stranger was playing a trick of some kind; Deering was confident of this and furious at his utter inability to cope with him. He clung to the back of a chair, trembling with anger.

"My name," the visitor continued, tossing his match into an ash-tray, "is Hood--R. Hood. The lone initial might suggest Robert or Roderigo, but if your nursery library was properly stocked you will recall a gentleman named Robin Hood of Sherwood Forest. I don't pretend to be a descendant--far from it; adopted the name out of sheer admiration for one of the grandest figures in all literature. Robin Hood, Don Quixote, and George Borrow are rubricated saints in my calendar. By the expression on your face I see that you don't make me out, and I can't blame you for thinking me insane; but, my dear boy, such an assumption does me a cruel wrong. Briefly, I'm a hobo with a weakness for good society, and yet a friend of the under dog. I confess to a passion for grand opera and lobster in all its forms. Do you grasp the idea?"

Deering did not grasp it. The man had protested his sanity, but Deering had heard somewhere that a confident belief in their mental soundness is a common hallucination of lunatics. Still, the stranger's steady gray eyes did not encourage the suspicion that he was mad. Deering's own reason, already severely taxed, was unequal to the task of dealing with this assured and cheerful Hood, who looked like a gentleman but talked like a fool.

"For God's sake, who are you and what do you want?" he demanded angrily.

Hood pushed him gently into a chair, utterly ignoring his fury.

"What time do we dine? Seven-thirty, I think your servant told me. I shan't dress if you don't mind. Speaking of clothes, that man of yours is a very superficial observer; let me in on the strength of my automobile coat, and I suppose the machine impressed him too. If he'd looked under the surface at these poor rags, I'd never have got by! That illustrates an ancient habit of the serving class in thinking all is gold that glitters. Snobs! Deplorable weakness! Let's talk like sensible men till the gong sounds."

Deering shook himself impatiently. This absurd talk, carefully calculated, he assumed, to prolong his misery, had torn his nerves to shreds. Hood sat down close to him in a straight-backed chair, crossed his legs, and thrust his hands into his coat pockets.

"My dear boy, in the name of all the gods at once, cheer up! To satisfy your very natural curiosity, I'll say that I fancied you were in trouble and needed a strong arm to sustain you in your hour of trial. Laudable purpose--ah, I see you begin to feel more comfortable. I have every intention of playing the big brother to you for a few hours, weeks, or months, or till you come out of your green funk. You wonder, of course, what motive I have for intruding in this way--lying to your servant, and making myself at home in your house. The motive, so far as there is any, is the purely selfish one of finding enjoyment for myself, while incidentally being of service to you. And you're bound to admit that that's a fair offer in this world of greed and selfishness. The great trouble with most of us is that the flavor so soon wears out of the chewing-gum. Do you remember the last time you had a good, hearty laugh? I'll wager you don't!"

Deering scowled, but Hood continued to expound his philosophy:

"The world's roaring along at such a rate we can't find happiness anywhere but in the dictionary. It's worrying me to death, just the spectacle of the fool old human race never getting a chance to sit down by the side of the road and pick the pebbles out of its shoes. Everybody's feet hurt and everybody's carrying a blood pressure that's bound to blow the roof off. I tell you, Deering, civilization hasn't got anything on the gypsies but soap and sanitary plumbing, I'm just forty-five and for years I've kept in motion most of the time. Alone of great travellers William Jennings Bryan has reviewed more water-tanks than I. I find the same delight in Butte, Peoria, Galesburg, Des Moines, Ashtabula, and Bangor, in Tallahassee, Birmingham, and Waco, that others seek in London, Paris, and Vienna--and it's all American stuff-- business of flags flying and Constitution being chanted offstage by a choir of a million voices! I've lived in coal-camps in Colorado, wintered with Maine lumbermen, hopped the ties with hobos, and enjoyed the friendship of thieves. I don't mean to brag, but I suppose there isn't a really first-rate crook in the country that I don't know. And down in the underworld they look on me--if I may modestly say it--as an old reliable friend. I've found these contacts immensely instructive, as you may imagine. Don't get nervous! I never stole anything in my life."

He thrust his fingers into his inside waistcoat pocket, and drew out a packet of bills, neatly folded, and opened them for Deering's wondering inspection.

"I beg of you don't jump to the conclusion that I roll in wealth. Money is poison to me; I hate the very smell of it--haven't a cent of my own in the world. This belongs to my chauffeur--carry it as a precaution merely."

Hood relighted his pipe, and dreamily watched the match blacken and curl in his fingers.

"Your chauffeur?" Deering suggested, like a child prompting a parent in the midst of an absorbing story.

"Oh, yes! Cassowary"--he pronounced the word lingeringly as though to prolong his pleasure in it--"real name doesn't matter. His father rolled up a big wad cutting the forest primeval into lumber, and left it to Cassowary--matter of a million or two. Cassowary had been driven to drink by an unhappy love-affair when I plucked him as a brand from burning Broadway. Nice chap, but too much self-indulgence; never had any discipline. He's pretty well broken in now, and as we seemed to need each other we follow the long trail together. Manage to hit it off first-rate. He's still mooning over the girl; tough that he can't have the only thing in the world he wants! Obstreperous parent adumbrated in the foreground, shotgun in hand. I don't allow Cassowary to carry any money--would rather risk contamination myself than expose him to it. If he stays with me for a few years, his accumulated income will roll up so that he can endow orchestras and art museums all through the prairie towns of the West, and become a great benefactor of mankind."

Hood's story was manifestly absurd, and yet he invested it with a certain plausibility. Even Cassowary, as Hood described him, seemed a wholly credible person, and the bills Hood had drawn from his pocket bore all the marks of honest money.

Dinner was announced, and Hood lounged down-stairs and into the dining-room arm in arm with Deering. A tapestry on the wall immediately attracted his attention. After pecking at the edges with his long, slender fingers he turned to his seat with a sigh.

"Preposterous imitation! I dare say it was passed off as a real Gobelin, but I know the artist who fakes those things--a New Jersey genius and very smooth at the game."

Deering had never paid the slightest attention to the tapestry, which had hung in the room for a dozen years, but he apologized in a vein of irony for its spuriousness, and steeled himself against complaints of the food; but after tasting the soup Hood praised it with enthusiasm. He was wholly at ease, and his table manners were beyond criticism. He seemed indifferent to the construction Deering or the bewildered Briggs might place upon his confessions, to which he now glibly addressed himself.

"A couple of years ago I was roaming through the Western provinces with a couple of old friends who persist--against my advice, I assure you--in the childish pastime of safe-blowing. We got pinched *en bloc*, and as I was broke I had to sponge on the yeggs to get me out of jail."

Briggs dropped a plate and Deering frowned at the interruption. Hood went on tranquilly:

"However, I was immured only three weeks, and the experience was broadening. That was in Omaha, and I'll say without fear of contradiction that the Omaha jail is one of the most comfortable in the Missouri Valley. I recommend it, Deering, without reservation, to any one in search of tranquillity. After they turned me loose I introduced myself to an old college classmate--fraternity brother--no danger of exposure. I had him put me up at the Omaha Club, and then I gave a dinner to the United States commissioner who heard my case, the district attorney, and the United States marshal. I wanted to ask the yeggs too--it seemed only square--but the judge was out of town, and the marshal was afraid his Honor might cite him for contempt if he brought his prisoners to my party. These things probably seem to you most banal, but take it all round I do manage to keep amused. Of course, now and then I pay more for my fun than it's worth. Last summer I mixed in with some moonshiners in Tennessee. Moonshining is almost a lost art, and I wanted the experience before the business became extinct. An unsociable lot, the lone still boys, and wouldn't warm up to me a bit. The unhappy result was a bullet through my left lung. I got patched up by a country doctor, but had to spend two months in a Philadelphia hospital for the finishing touches."

Deering's uneasiness increased. This man who spoke so blithely of imprisonment and bullets in his lung must have a motive for his visit. With a jerk of the head he sent Briggs from the room.

"This is all very amusing," he remarked with decision as he put down his salad-fork, "but will you pardon me for asking just why you came here? I have your own word for it that your favorite amusement is consorting with criminals, and that money you flashed may have been stolen for all I know! If you have any business with me----"

"My dear boy, I don't blame you for growing restless," replied Hood amiably. "Of course, I know that your father and sister are away, and that you are alone. Your family history I am pretty familiar with; your antecedents and connections are excellent. Your mother, who died four years ago, was of the Rhode Island Ranger family--and there is no better blood in America. Your sister Constance won the Westchester golf championship last year--I learned that from the newspapers, which I read with a certain passion, as you have observed. If I hadn't thought you needed company--my company particularly--I shouldn't have landed on your door-step. You dined Monday night at the Hotel Pendragon--at a table in the corner on the Fifth Avenue side, and your dejection touched me deeply. Afterward you went down to the rathskeller, and sat there all alone drinking stuff you didn't need. It roused my apprehensions. I feared things were going badly with you, and I thought I'd give you a chance to unburden your soul to me, Hood, the enchanted hobo----"

"For sheer cheek--" began Deering hotly.

Hood lifted his hand deprecatingly.

"Please don't!" he remarked soothingly. "With the tinkle of a bell you can call your man and have me bounced. I repacked my bag after taking a bath in your very comfortable guest-room, and we can part immediately. But let us be sensible, Deering; just between ourselves, don't you really need me?"

His tone was ingratiating, his manner the kindest. Deering had walked the streets for two days trying to bring himself to the point of confessing his plight to one of a score of loyal friends--men he had known from prep-school days, and on through college: active, resourceful, wealthy young fellows who would risk much to help him--and yet in his fear and misery he had shrunk from approaching them. Hood, he was now convinced, was not a detective come to arrest him; in fact his guest's sympathies and connections seemed to lie on the other side of the law's bar-ricade.

They had coffee in the living-room, where Hood, inspired by specimens of the work of several of the later French painters, discussed art with sophistication. Deering observed him intently. There was something immensely attractive in Hood's face; his profile, clean-cut as a cameo, was thoroughly masculine; his head was finely moulded, and his gray eyes were frank and responsive.

"It's possible," said Deering, after a long silence in which Hood smoked meditatively, "that you may be able to help me."

On a sudden impulse he rose and put out his hand.

"Thank you," said Hood gravely, "but don't tell me unless you really want to."

II

So after all the bother of stealing two hundred thousand dollars' worth of negotiable securities you *lost* them!" Hood remarked when Deering ended his recital.

Deering frowned and nodded. Not only had he told his story to this utter stranger, but he had found infinite relief in doing so.

"Let us go over the points again," said Hood calmly. "You set down your suitcase containing two hundred K. & L. Terminal 5's in the Grand Central Station, turned round to buy a ticket to Boston, and when you picked up the bag it was the wrong one! Such instances are not rare; the strong family resemblance between suitcases has caused much trouble in this world. Only the other day a literary friend told me the magazine editors have placed a ban on mixed suitcases as a fictional device; but of course that doesn't help us any in this affair. I've known a few professional suitcase lifters. One of the smoothest is Sammy Tibbots, but he's doing time in Joliet, so we may as well eliminate Sammy."

"No, no!" Deering exclaimed impatiently. "It was a girl who did the trick! She was at the local ticket window, just behind me. You see, I was nervous and after I bought my ticket it dropped to the floor, and while I was picking it up that girl grabbed my suitcase and beat it for the gate."

"Enter the girl," Hood muttered. "'Twas ever thus! Of course, you telegraphed ahead and stopped her--that was the obvious course."

"There you go! If I'd done that, there wouldn't have been any publicity; oh, no!" Deering replied contemptuously. "People don't carry big bunches of bonds around in suitcases; they send 'em by registered express. Of course, if the girl was honest she'd report the matter to the railroad officials and they'd notify the police, and they'd be looking for the thief! And that's just what I don't want."

"Of course not," Hood assented readily. "That was Wednesday and this is Friday, and you haven't seen any ads in the papers about a suitcase full of bonds? Well, I'd hardly have missed such a thing myself. What did the girl look like?"

"Small, dressed in blue and wearing a white veil. She made a lively sprint for the gate, and climbed into the last car just as the train started. The conductor yelled to her not to try it, but the porter jumped out and pushed her up the steps."

At Hood's suggestion Deering brought the suitcase that had been exchanged for his own, and disclosed its contents--a filmy night-dress, a silk shirt-waist, a case of ivory toilet articles bearing a complicated monogram, a bottle of violet-water, half empty, a pair of silk stockings, a novel, a pair of patent-leather pumps, all tumbled together.

"The young person left in haste, that's clear enough," remarked Hood, balancing one of the pumps in his hand. "'Bonet, Paris,'" he read, squinting at the lining. "Most deplorable that we have both slippers; one would have been a clew, and we could have spent the rest of our lives measuring footprints. Very nice slippers, though; fastidious young person, I'll wager. The monogram on these trinkets is of no assistance--it might be R. G. T., or T. G. R., or G. R. T. Monograms are a nuisance, a delusion, a snare!"

Deering flung the faintly scented violet-tinted toilet-case into the bag resentfully.

"The silly little fool; why didn't she mind what she was doing!" he exclaimed angrily, "and not steal other people's things!"

"Pardon me," Hood remonstrated, "but from your story the less you speak of stealing the better. But it isn't clear yet why you sneaked the bonds. Your father has a reputation for generosity; you're an only son and slated to succeed him in the banking-house. Just what was your idea in starting for Boston with the loot?"

"It was to help Ned Ranscomb, an old pal of mine," Deering blurted--"one of the best fellows on earth, who has pulled me out of a lot of holes. He'd taken options on Mizpah Copper for more than he could pay for and fell on my neck to help him out. And the rotten part of it is that I can't find him anywhere! I've telephoned and telegraphed all over creation, but he's fallen off the earth! I tell you everything from the start has gone wrong. I guess I didn't tell you that I already had a couple of hundred thousand in Mizpah--all I could put up personally, and now I've lost the two hundred thousand I stole, and Ned's got cold feet and drowned himself, and here I'm talking about it to a man who may be a crook for all I know!"

"This disappearance of Ranscomb has a suspicious look," remarked Hood, ignoring the fling. "Either money or a woman, of course."

"Ranscomb," Deering retorted savagely, "is all business and never fools with women. And you can bet that with this big copper deal on he wouldn't waste time on any girl that ever was born."

"Human beings are as we find them," observed Hood judicially, "but you're entirely too tragic about this whole business. If it isn't comedy, it's nothing. I'll wager the girl who skipped with your stolen boodle has a sense of humor. The key-note to her character is in this novel she grabbed as she hastily packed her bag--'The Madness of May.' That's one of the drollest books ever written. A story like that is a boon to mankind; it kept me chuckling all night. Haven't read it? Well, the heroine excused herself from a dinner-table that was boring her to death, ran to her room and packed a suitcase, and that was the last her friends saw of her for some time. Along about this season it's in the blood of healthy human beings to pine for clean air and the open road. It's the wanderlust that's in all of us, old and young alike. It's possible that the young lady who ran off with your bonds felt the spring madness and determined to hit the trail as the girl did in that yarn. Finding herself possessed of a lot of bonds belonging to a stranger, I dare say she is badly frightened. Put yourself in that girl's place, Deering--imagine her feelings, landing somewhere after a hurried journey, opening her suitcase to chalk her nose, and finding herself a thief!"

"Rot!" sniffed Deering angrily.

One moment he distrusted Hood; the next his heart warmed to him. At the table the light-hearted adventurer had kept him entertained and amused with his running comment on books, public characters, the world's gold supply, and scrapes he had been in, without dropping any clew to his identity. He seemed to be a veritable encyclopaedia of places; apparently there was not a town in the United States that he hadn't visited, and he spoke of exclusive clubs and thieves' dens in the same breath. But Deering's hopes of gaining practical aid in the search for the lost bonds was rapidly waning.

"There's no use being silly about this; I'm going to telephone to a detective agency and tell them to send out a good man, right away--to-night----"

"As you please," Hood assented, "but if you do, you'll regret it to your last hour. I know the whole breed, and you may count on their making a mess of it. And consider for a moment that what you propose means putting a hired bloodhound on the trail of a girl who probably never harmed a kitten in her life. It would be rotten caddishness to send a policeman after her. It isn't done, Deering; it isn't done! Of course, there's not much chance that the sleuths would ever come within a hundred miles of her, but what if they found her! You are a gentleman, Deering, and that's not the game for you to play."

"Then tell me a better one! In ten days at the farthest father will be back and what am I going to say to him--how am I going to explain breaking into his safety box and stealing those bonds?"

"You can't explain it, of course, and it's rather up to you, son, to put 'em back. Every hour you spend talking about it is wasted time. That girl's had your suitcase two days, and it's your duty to find her. Something must have happened or she'd have turned it back to the railroad company. Perhaps she's been arrested as a thief and thrown into jail! Again, her few effects point to a degree of prosperity--she's not a girl who would steal for profit; I'll swear to that. We must find that girl! We'll toss a slipper and start off the way the toe points."

Indifferent to Deering's snort of disgust, Hood was already whirling the slipper in the air.

"Slightly northeast! There you are, Deering--the clear pointing of Fate! The girl wasn't going far or she wouldn't have been in the local ticket line, and even a lady in haste packs more stuff for a long journey. We'll run up to the Barton Arms--an excellent inn, and establish headquarters. The girl who danced off with your two hundred thousand is probably around there somewhere, bringing up her tennis for the first tournaments of the season. Let's be moving; a breath of air will do you good."

"That's all you can do about it, is it?" demanded Deering. "Let me tell my whole story--put myself in your power, and now the best you can do is to flip a slipper to see which way to start!"

"Just as good a way as any," remarked Hood amiably.

He pressed the button, ordered his car, and then led the way back to Deering's room.

"Throw some things into a bag. You'll soon forget your sordid money affairs and begin to live, and you'd better be prepared for anything that turns up. I'll fold the coats; some old fishing-togs for rough work and jails, and even your dress suit may come in handy."

He fell to work, folding the suits neatly, while Deering moved about like a man in a trance, assembling linen and toilet articles.

"Something tells me we're going to have a pretty good time," continued Hood musingly. "I'll show you untold kingdoms, things that never were on sea or land. We shall meet people worn with the world-old struggle for things they don't need, and who are out in the tender May air looking for happiness--the only business, my dear boy, that's really worth while. And you'll be surprised, son, to find how many such people there are."

"Ah, you're ready, Cassowary!" remarked Hood as they stepped out of the side door where a big touring-car was drawn up in the driveway. "Just a moment till I get my stick."

Briggs had placed their bags in the car, and Deering had a moment in which to observe the chauffeur, who stood erect and touched his cap. Hood's protege proved to be a tall, dark, well-knit young fellow dressed in a well-fitting chauffeur's costume.

"It's a good night for a run," Deering suggested, eying the man in the light from the door.

"Fine, sir."

"I hope the people in the house took good care of you."

"Very good, sir."

There was nothing in Cassowary's voice or manner to indicate that he was the possessor of the fortune to which Hood had referred so lightly. Deering's hastily formed impressions of Hood's chauffeur were wholly agreeable and satisfying.

Hood, lingering in the hall, could be heard warning Briggs against the further accumulation of fat. He recommended a new system of reducing, and gave the flushed and stuttering butler the name of a New York specialist in dietetics whom he advised him to consult without delay.

The chauffeur's lips twitched and, catching Deering's eye, he winked. Deering tapped his forehead. Cassowary shook his head.

"Don't you believe it!" he ejaculated with spirit.

At this moment Hood appeared on the steps, banging his recovered stick noisily as he descended.

"The Barton Arms, Cassowary," he ordered, and they set off at a lively clip.

III

On the steps of the Barton Arms an hour later Hood and Deering ran into two men who were just leaving the inn. Hood greeted them heartily as old acquaintances and remained talking to them while Deering went to ask for rooms.

"The suspicions of those fellows always tickle me," he remarked as he joined Deering at the desk, where he scrawled "R. Hood, Sherwoodville," on the register. "Detectives--rather good as the breed goes, but not men of true vision. Now and then I've been able to give them a useful hint--the slightest, mind you, and only where I could divert suspicion from some of my friends in the underworld. I always try to be of assistance to predatory genius; there are clever crooks and stupid ones; the kind who stoop to vulgar gun-work when their own stupidity gets them into a tight pinch don't appeal to me. My artistic sensibilities are affronted by clumsy work."

"Perhaps--" Deering suggested with a hasty glance at the door--"maybe they're looking for me!"

"Bless you, no," Hood replied as they followed a boy with their bags; "nothing so intelligent as that. On the contrary"--he paused at the landing and laid his hand impressively on Deering's arm--"on the contrary, they're looking for *me*!"

He went on with a chuckle and a shake of the head, as though the thought of being pursued by detectives gave him the keenest pleasure. When he reached their rooms he sat down and struck his knee sharply and chuckled again. Deering turned frowningly for an explanation of his mirth.

"Oh, don't bother about those chaps! I repeat, that they are looking for me, but"--he knit his fingers behind his head and grinned--"they don't **know** it!"

"Don't know you are you!" exclaimed Deering.

"You never said a truer word! More than that, they're not likely to! There are things, son, I--Hood, the frankest of mortals--can't tell even you! I, Hood, the inexplicable; Hood, the prince of tramps, the connoisseur in all the arts--even I must have my secrets; but in time, my dear boy, in time you shall know everything! But there's work before us! The long arm of coincidence beckons us. We shall test for ourselves all the claptrap of the highest-priced novelists."

Deering walked to the window and stared out at the landscape, then strode toward Hood angrily.

"I don't like this!" he wailed despairingly. "You promised to help me find those stolen bonds, and now you're talking like a lunatic again. If I can't find the bonds, I've got to find Ranscomb, and get back that first two hundred thousand I gave him. I can't stand this--detectives waiting for us wherever we stop, and you babbling rot--rot--" Words failed him; he clinched his hands and glared.

"Don't bluster, son, or I shall grow peevish," Hood replied tolerantly. "At the present moment I feel like taking a walk under the mystical May stars. The night invites the soul to meditation; the stars may have the answer to all our perplexities. Stop fretting about your bonds and your friend Ranscomb; very likely he's busted, clean broke; that's what usually happens to fellows who take money from their friends and put it into the metals. Possibly he swallowed poison, and went to sleep forever just to escape your wrath. Let us take counsel of the heavens and try to forget your sins. We must still move the way the slipper pointed--northeast. The road bends away from the inn just right for a fresh start. We depart, we skip, we are on our way, my dear boy!"

They had walked nearly a mile when Deering announced that he was tired, and refused to go farther. He clambered upon a stone wall at the roadside. On a high ridge some distance away and etched against the stars was a long, low house.

"Splendid type of bungalow," Hood commented, throwing his legs over the wall. "I'm glad you have an eye for nice effects--the roof makes a pretty line against the stars, and those pines beyond add a touch--a distinct touch. Bungalows should always be planned with a view to night effects; too bad architects don't always consider little points like that."

Deering growled angrily. Suddenly as his eyes gazed over the long, sloping meadow that rose to the house he started and laid his hand on Hood's knee.

"Steady, steady! Always give a ghost a chance," murmured Hood.

If the figure that danced across the meadow was a ghost, it was an agile one, and its costume represented a radical departure from the traditional garb of spirits doomed to walk the night.

"A boy, kicking up before he goes to bed," suggested Deering, forgetting his sorrows for the moment as he contemplated the dancing apparition.

"In a clown's suit, if I'm any judge," said Hood, jumping down from the wall and moving cautiously up the slope. The dancing figure suddenly darted away through a clump of trees.

"Of course," remarked Hood when they had reached the level where the figure had executed its fantastic gyrations, "of course, it's none of our affair; but, in that story I was telling you about, the heroine danced around at night in strange costumes scaring people to death. I'm not saying this ghost has read that book--I'm merely stating a fact."

They found a path that zigzagged across the meadow and followed it to the edge of a ravine. Below they heard the ripple of running water; and as an agreeable accompaniment some one was whistling softly.

In a moment the rattle of loosened gravel caused them to drop down by the path. The pantalooned figure came up, still whistling, and paused for a moment to take breath. Deering, throwing himself back from the path, grasped a bush. The twigs rattled noisily, and with a frightened "Oh!" the clown darted away, nimbly and fleetly. They followed a white blur in the starlight for an instant and heard the patter of light feet.

"A girl," whispered Deering.

"I believe you are right," remarked Hood, feeling about in the grass, "and here's a part of her costume." He picked up something white and held it to his face. "She dropped her clown's cap when you began shaking the scenery. I seem to remember that a girl's hair is sweet like that! In old times the clown's cap was supposed to possess magic. Son, we have begun well! A girl masquerading, happy victim of the May madness--this is the jolliest thing I've struck in years--a girl, out dancing all by her lonesome under the stars--Columbine playing Harlequin!"

"We might as well be off," he added, relighting his pipe. "We frightened her ladyship, and she will dance no more to-night. However, we have her cap, which points the way for to-morrow's work."

"You're going to hang around here watching a girl cut monkey-shines!" moaned Deering. "You haven't forgotten what we're looking for, have you!" he demanded, shaking his fist in Hood's face.

"Once more, be calm! Don't you see that you're on the verge of a new 'Midsummer Night's Dream'; that the world's tired of work and gone back to play! Don't talk like a tired business man whose wife has dragged him to see one of Ibsen's frolics--'Rosmersholm,' for example--where they talk for three hours and then jump in the well! The fact that there's one girl left in the world to dance under stars ought to hearten you for anything. We don't find in this world the things we're looking for, Deering; we've got to be ready for surprises. I won't say that that's the girl who ran off with your bonds; all I can say is that she's as likely to be the one as any girl I can think of. Tut! Don't imagine I don't sympathize with you in your troubles; but forget them, that's the ticket. This will do for to-night. We'd better go back to the Barton and to bed."

He yawned sleepily and started toward the road. Deering caught him by the arm.

"I was just thinking--" he began.

"Thinking is a bad habit, my boy. Thought is the curse of the world. The less thinking we do the better off we are. Down at Pass Christian last winter I sat under a tree for a solid month and never thought a think. Most profitable time I ever spent in my life. Camped with a sneak-thief who was making a tour of the Southern resorts--nice chap; must tell you about him sometime."

He chuckled as though the recollection of his larcenous companion pleased him tremendously.

"I don't believe I'll go back to the Barton just yet," Deering suggested timidly. "It's possible, you know, that that girl **might**----"

"You've got it!" exclaimed Hood eagerly, clapping his hands upon Deering's shoulders. "The spell is taking hold! Wait here a thousand years if you like for that kid to come back, and don't bother about me. But cut out your vulgar bond twaddle, and don't ask her if she stole your suitcase! As like as not she'll lead you to the end of the rainbow, and show you a meal sack bulging with red, red gold. Here's her cap--better keep it for good luck."

Deering stood, with the clown's cap in his hand, staring after Hood's retreating figure. It was not wholly an illusion that he had experienced a change of some sort, and he wondered whether there might not be something in Hood's patter about the May madness. At any rate, his troubles had slipped from him, and he was conscious of a new and delightful sense of freedom. Moreover, he had been kidnapped by the oddest man he had ever met, and he didn't care!

IV

Beyond the bungalow rose a dark strip of woodland, and suddenly, as Deering's eyes caught sight of it, he became aware that the moon, which had not appeared before that night, seemed to be lingering cosily among the trees. Even a victim of May madness hardly sees moons where they do not exist, but to all intents and purpose this *was* a moon, a large round moon, on its way down the horizon in the orderly fashion of elderly moons. He turned toward the road, then glanced back quickly to make sure his eyes were not playing tricks upon him. The moon was still there, blandly staring. His powers of orientation had often been tested; on hunting and fishing trips he had ranged the wilderness without a compass, and never come to grief. He was sure that this huge orb was in the north, where no moon of decent habits has any right to be.

With his eyes glued to this phenomenon, he advanced up the slope. When he reached the crest of the meadow the moon still hung where he had first seen it--a most unaccountable moon that apparently lingered to encourage his investigations.

He jumped a wall that separated the meadow from the woodland, and advanced resolutely toward the lunar mystery. He found Stygian darkness in among the pines: the moon, considering its size, shed amazingly little light. He crept toward it warily, and in a moment stood beneath the outward and visible form of a moon cleverly contrived of barrel staves and tissue-paper with a lighted lantern inside, and thrust into the crotch of a tree.

As he contemplated it something struck him--something, he surmised, that had been flung by mortal hand, and a pine-cone caught in his waistcoat collar.

"Please don't spoil my moon," piped a voice out of the darkness. "It's a lot of trouble to make a moon!"

Walking cautiously toward the wall, he saw, against the star dusk of the open, the girl in clown costume who had danced in the meadow. She sat the long way of the wall, her knees clasped comfortably, and seemed in nowise disturbed by his appearance.

"I beg your pardon," he said, "but I didn't know it was *your* moon. I thought it was just the regular old moon that had got lost on the way home."

"Oh, don't apologize. I rather hoped somebody would come up to have a look at it; but you'd better run along now. This is private property, you know."

"Thanks for the hint," he remarked. "But on a night when moons hang in trees you can't expect me to be scared away so easily. And besides, I'm an outlaw," he ended in a tone meant to be terrifying.

She betrayed neither surprise nor fear, but laughed and uttered a "Really!" that was just such a "really" as any well-bred girl might use at a tea, or anywhere else that reputable folk congregate, to express faint surprise. Her way of laughing was altogether charming. A girl who donned a clown's garb for night prowling and manufactured moons for her own amusement could not have laughed otherwise, he reflected.

"A burglar?" she suggested with mild curiosity.

"Not professionally; but I'm seriously thinking of going in for it. What do you think of burgling as a career?"

"Interesting--rather--I should think," she replied after a moment's hesitation, as though she were weighing his suggestion carefully.

"And highway robbery appeals to me--rather. It's more picturesque, and you wouldn't have to break into houses. I think I'd rather work in the open."

"The chances of escape might be better," she admitted; "but you needn't try the bungalow down there, for there's nothing in it worth stealing. I give you my word for that!"

"Oh, I hadn't thought of the bungalow. I had it in mind to begin by holding up a motor. Nobody's doing that sort of thing just now."

"Capital!" she murmured pleasantly, as though she found nothing extraordinary in the idea. "So you're really new at the game."

"Well, I've *stolen* before, if that's what you mean, but I didn't get much fun out of it. I suppose after the first fatal plunge the rest will come easier."

"I dare say that's true," she assented. There was real witchery in the girl's light, murmurous laugh.

It seemed impossible to surprise her; she was taking him as a matter of course-- as though sitting on a wall at night, and talking to a strange young man about steal- ing was a familiar experience.

"I've joined Robin Hood's band," he continued. "At least I've been adopted by a new sort of Robin Hood who's travelling round robbing the rich to pay the poor, and otherwise meddling in people's affairs--the old original Robin Hood brought up to date. If it hadn't been for him I might be cooling my heels in jail right now. He's an expert on jails--been in nearly every calaboose in America. He's tucked me un- der his wing--persuaded me to take the highway, and not care a hang for anything."

"How delightful!" she replied, but so slowly that he began to fear that his con- fidences had alarmed her. "That's too good to be true; you're fooling, aren't you-- really?"

His eyes had grown accustomed to the light, and her profile was now faintly limned in the dusk. Hers was the slender face of youth. The silhouette revealed the straightest of noses and the firmest of little chins. She was young, so young that he felt himself struggling in an immeasurable gulf of years as he watched her. Appar- ently such sophistication as she possessed was in the things of the world of wonder, the happy land of make-believe.

"Keats would have liked a night like this," she said gently.

Deering was silent. Keats was a person whom he knew only as the subject of a tiresome lecture in his English course at college.

"Bill Blake would have adored it, but he would have had lambs in the pasture," she added.

"Bill Blake?" he questioned. "Do you mean Billy Blake who was half-back on the Harvard eleven last year?"

She tossed her head and laughed merrily.

"I love that!" she replied lingeringly, as though to prolong her joy in his igno- rance. "I was thinking of a poet of that name who wrote a nice verse something like this:

'I give you the end of a golden string;
Only wind it into a ball,
It will lead you in at Heaven's gate,
Built in Jerusalem's wall.'"

No girl had ever quoted poetry to him before, and he was thinking more of her pretty way of repeating the stanza--keeping time with her hands--than of the verse itself.

"Well," he said, "what's the rest of it?"

"Oh, there isn't any rest of it! Don't you see that there couldn't be anything more--that it's finished--a perfect little poem all by itself!"

He played with a loosened bit of stone, meekly conscious of his stupidity. And he did not like to appear stupid before a girl who danced alone in the starlight and hung moons in trees.

"I'm afraid I don't get it. I'd a lot rather stay by this wall talking to you than go to Jerusalem."

"You'd be foolish to do that if you really had the end of the golden string, and could follow it to Paradise. I think it means any nice place--just any place where happiness is."

He was not getting on, and to gain time he bade her repeat the stanza.

"I think I understand now; I've never gone in much for poetry, you know," he explained humbly.

"Burglars are natural poets, I suppose," she continued. "A burglar just has to have imagination or he can't climb through the window of a house he has never seen before. He must imagine everything perfectly--the silver on the sideboard, the watch under the pillow, and the butler stealing down the back stairs with a large, shiny pistol in his hand."

"Certainly," Deering agreed readily. "And if he runs into a policeman on the way out he's got to imagine that it's an old college friend and embrace him."

"You mustn't spoil a pretty idea that way!" she admonished in a tone that greatly softened the rebuke. "Come to think of it, you haven't told me your name yet; of course, if you become a burglar, you will have a great number of names, but I'd like awfully to know your true one."

"Why?" he demanded.

"Because you seem nice and well brought up for a burglar, and I liked your going up to the moon and poking your finger into it. That makes me feel that I'd like to know you."

"Well, the circumstances being as they are, and being really a thief, you mustn't ask me to tell my real name; for all I know you may be a detective in disguise."

"I'm not--really," she said--he found her "reallys" increasingly enchanting.

"You might call me Friar Tuck or Little John. I'm travelling with Robin Hood, you remember."

"Mr. Tuck--that will be splendid!"

"And now that you know my name it's only fair to tell me yours."

"Pierrette," she answered.

"Not really!"

His unconscious imitation of her manner of uttering this phrase evoked another merry laugh.

"Yes, really," she answered.

"And you live somewhere, of course--not in the tree up there with your moon, but in the bungalow, I suppose."

"I live wherever I am; that's the fun of playing all the time," she replied evasively. "***Poste restante***, the Little Dipper. How do you like that?"

"But just now your true domicile is the bungalow?" he persisted.

"Oh, I've been stopping there for a few days, that's all. I haven't any home--not really," she added as though she found her homelessness the happiest of conditions. She snapped her fingers and recited:

"Wherever stars shine brightest, there my home shall be,
In the murmuring forest or by the sounding sea,
With overhead the green bough and underfoot the grass,
Where only dreams and butterflies ever dare to pass!"

"Is that Keats or Blake?" he ventured timidly.

"It's ***me***, you goose! But it's only an imitation--why, Stevenson, of course, and pretty punk as you ought to know. Gracious!"

She jumped down from the wall, on the side toward the bungalow, and stared up at the tree she had embellished with her moon.

"The moon's gone out, and I've got to go *in*!"

"Please, before you go, when can I see you again?"

"Who knows!" she exclaimed unsympathetically; but she waited as though pondering the matter.

"But I must see you again!" he persisted.

"Oh, I shouldn't say that it was wholly essential to your happiness--or mine! I can't meet burglars--socially!"

"Burglars! But I'm not--" he cried protestingly.

She bent toward him with one hand extended pleadingly.

"Don't say it! Don't *say* it! If you say you're *not*, you won't be any fun any more!"

"Well, then we'll say I am--a terrible freebooter--a bold, bad pirate," he growled. "Now, may I come?"

She mused a moment, then struck her hands together.

"Come to the bungalow breakfast; that's a fine idea!"

"And may I bring Hood?" he asked, leaning half-way across the wall in his anxiety to conclude the matter before she escaped. "He's my boss, you understand, and I'm afraid I can't shake him."

"Certainly; bring Mr. Hood. Breakfast at eight."

"And your home--your address--is there in the bungalow?"

"I've told you where my home is, in a verse I made up specially; and my address is care of the Little Dipper--there it is, up there in the sky, all nice and silvery."

His gaze followed the pointing of her finger. The Little Dipper, as an address for the use of mortals, struck him as rather remote. To his surprise she advanced to the wall, rested her hands upon it, and peered into his face.

"Isn't this perfectly killing?" she asked in a tone wholly different from that in which she had carried on her share of the colloquy.

He experienced an agreeable thrill as it flashed upon him that this was no child, but a young woman who, knowing the large world, had suddenly awakened to a consciousness that encounters with strange young men by starlight were not to be prolonged forever. In the luminous dusk he noted anew the delicate perfectness of her face, the fine brow about which her hair had tumbled from her late exertions. Her eyes searched his face with honest curiosity--for an instant only.

Then she stepped back, as though to mark a return to her original character, and answered her own question with an air of amused conviction:

"It *is* perfectly killing!"

His hand fumbled the cap in his pocket.

"Here's something I found down yonder--your clown's cap."

She took it with a murmur of thanks, and darted away toward the bungalow. He heard her light step on the veranda and then a door closed with a sharp bang.

Deering walked back to the inn with his head high and elation throbbing in his pulses. He observed groups of people playing bridge in the inn parlor, and he was filled with righteous contempt for them. The May air had changed his whole nature. He was not the William B. Deering who had meditated killing himself a few hours earlier. A new joy had entered into him; he was only afraid now that he might not live forever!

Hood slept tranquilly, his bed littered with the afternoon's New York papers which evidently he had been scissoring when he fell asleep. Deering's attitude toward the strange vagrant had changed since his meeting with Pierrette. Hood might be as mad as the traditional hatter, and yet there was something--indubitably something--about the man that set him apart from the common run of mortals.

Deering lay awake a long time rejoicing in his new life, and when he dreamed it was of balloon-like moons cruising lazily over woods and fields, pursued by innumerable Pierrettes in spotted trousers and pointed caps.

V

He awoke at seven, and looked in upon Hood, who lay sprawled upon his bed reading one of the battered volumes of Borrow he carried in his bag. "Get your tub, son; I've had mine and came back to bed to let you have your sleep out. Marvellous man--Borrow. Spring's the time to read him. We'll have some breakfast and go out and see what the merry old world has to offer."

With nice calculation he tossed the book into the open bag on the further side of the room, rose, and stretched himself. Deering stifled an impulse to scoff at his silk pajamas as hardly an appropriate sleeping garb for one who professed to have taken vows of poverty. Hood noted his glance.

"Found these in some nabob's house at Bar Harbor last fall. Went up in November, after all the folks had gone, to have a look at the steely blue ocean; camped in a big cottage for a few days. Found a drawer full of these things and took the pink ones. Wrote my thanks on the villa's stationery and pinned 'em to the fireplace. I hate to admit it, son, but I verily believe I could stand a little breakfast."

"We're going out for breakfast," Deering remarked with affected carelessness. "I accepted an invitation for you last night. A girl up there at the bungalow asked me; I told her about you, and she seemed willing to stand for it."

"The thought pleases me! You are certainly doing well, my boy!" Hood replied, dancing about on one foot as he drew a sock on the other.

He explained that a man should never sit down while dressing; that the exercise he got in balancing himself was of the greatest value as a stimulus to the circulation.

"She's a very nice girl, I think," Deering continued, showing his lathered face at the bathroom door.

He hadn't expected Hood to betray surprise, and he was not disappointed in the matter-of-course fashion in which his companion received the invitation.

"Breakfast is the one important meal of the day," Hood averred as he executed a series of hops in his efforts to land inside his trousers. "All great adventures should be planned across breakfast tables; centrepiece of cool fruits; coffee of teasing fragrance, the toast crisp; an egg perhaps, if the morning labors are to be severe. I know a chap in Boston who cuts out breakfast altogether. Most melancholy person I ever knew; peevish till one o'clock, then throws in a heavy lunch that ruins him for the rest of the day. What did you say the adorable's name was?"

"Pierrette," Deering spluttered from the tub.

"Delightful!" cried Hood, flourishing his hair-brushes. "Then you met the dancing-girl! I must say----"

"She had hung a moon in a tree! I followed the moon and found the girl!"

"Always the way; it never fails," Hood commented, as though the finding of the girl had fully justified his philosophy of life. "But we can't fool away much time at the bungalow; we've got a lot to do to-day."

"Time!" cried Deering, "I'm going to stay forever! You can't expect me to find a girl whose post-office address is the Little Dipper, and then go coolly off and forget about her!"

"That's the right spirit, son," Hood remarked cautiously; "but we'll see. I'll have a look at her and decide what's best for you. My business right now is to keep you out of trouble. You can't tell about these moon girls; she may have a wart on her nose when you see her in daylight."

Deering hooted.

"And she probably has parents who may not relish the idea of having two strange men prowling about the premises looking for breakfast. There are still a few of those old-fashioned people left in the world. It may be only a backdoor hand-out for us, but I've sawed wood for breakfast before now. I'll wait for you below; I want to see how old Cassowary's standing the racket. The boy seemed a little cheerfuller last night."

They walked to the bungalow which, to Deering's relief, was still perched on the ridge as he had left it. He was beset with misgivings as they entered the gate and followed a hedge-lined path that rose gradually to the house; it might be a joke after all; but Hood's manner was reassuring. He swung his stick and praised the landscape, and when they reached the veranda banged the knocker noisily. A capped and aproned maid opened the door immediately.

Deering, struck with cowardice, found his legs quaking and stepped back to allow Hood to declare their purpose.

"We have come for breakfast, lass," Hood announced, "and have brought our appetites with us if that fact interests you."

"You are expected," said the maid; "breakfast will be served immediately."

She led the way across a long living-room to the dining-room beyond, where a table was set for three. The tangible presence of the third plate caused Deering's heart to thump.

"The host or hostess--?" Hood inquired as the girl waited for them to be seated.

"The lady of the house wished me to say that she would be here--in spirit! Pressing duties called her elsewhere."

Deering's spirits sank. Pierrette, then, was only a dream of the night, and had never had the slightest intention of meeting him at breakfast! The maid curtsied and vanished through a swing door.

Hood, accepting the situation as he found it, expressed his satisfaction as a bowl of strawberries was placed on the table, and as the door ceased swinging behind the maid, laid his hand on Deering's arm. "Don't worry; mere shyness has driven our divinity away: you can see for yourself that even a girl who hangs moons in trees might shrink from the shock of a daylight meeting with a gentleman she had found amusing by starlight. Let it suffice that she provided the breakfast according to schedule--that's highly encouraging. With strawberries at present prices she has been generous. This little disappointment merely adds zest to the adventure."

The hand of the maid as she changed his plate at once interested Deering. It was a slender, supple, well-kept hand, browned by the sun. Her maid's dress was becoming; her cap merely served to invite attention to her golden-brown hair. Her coloring left nothing for the heart to desire, and her brown eyes called immediately for a second glance. She was deft and quick; her graceful walk in itself compelled admiration. As the door closed upon her, Hood bent a look of inquiry upon his brooding companion.

"Perhaps she's the adorable--the true, authentic Pierrette," he suggested.

Deering shook his head.

"No; the other girl was not so tall and her voice was different; it was wonderfully sweet and full of laughter. I couldn't be fooled about it."

"There's mystery here--a game of some kind. Mark the swish of silken skirts; unless my eyes fail me, I caught a glimpse of silken hose as she flitted into the pantry."

When an omelet had been served and the coffee poured (she poured coffee charmingly!) Hood called her back as she was about to leave them.

"Two men should never be allowed to eat alone. If your mistress is not returning at once, will you not do us the honor to sit down with us?"

"Thank you, sir," she said, biting her lip to conceal a smile.

Deering was on his feet at once and drew out the third chair, which she accepted without debate. She composedly folded her arms on the edge of the table as though she were in nowise violating the rules set down for the guidance of waitresses. Hood, finding the situation to his taste, blithely assumed the lead in the conversation.

"It is perfectly proper for you to join us at table," he remarked, "but formal introductions would not be in keeping. Still, your employer doubtless has some familiar name for you, and you might with propriety tell us what it is, so we won't need to attract your attention by employing the vulgar 'Say' or 'Listen'!"

"My mistress calls me Babette," she answered, her lashes drooping becomingly.

"Perfect!" cried Hood ecstatically. "And we are two outlaws whose names it is more discreet for us to withhold, even if it were proper to exchange names with a mere housemaid."

Deering winced; it was indecent in Hood to treat her as though she were a housemaid when so obviously she was not.

"My friend doesn't mean to be rude," he explained; "the morning air always makes him a little delirious."

"I hope I know my place," the girl replied, "and I'm sure you gentlemen mean to be kind."

"You needn't count the spoons after we leave," said Hood; "I assure you we have no professional designs on the house."

"Thank you, sir. Of course, if you stole anything, it would be taken out of my wages."

Deering's interest in her increased.

She rested her chin on her hand just as his sister often did when they lingered together at table. He was a good brother and Constance was his standard. He was sure that Constance would like Pierrette's maid. He resented Hood's patronizing attitude toward the girl, but Hood's spirits were soaring and there was no checking him.

"Babette," he began, "I'm going to trouble you with a question, not doubting you will understand that my motives are those of a philosopher whose whole life has been devoted to the study of the human race. May I ask you to state in all sincerity whether you consider apple sauce the essential accompaniment of roast duck?"

"I do not; nor do I care for jelly with venison," she answered readily.

"Admirable! You are clearly no child of convention but an independent thinker! May I smoke? Thanks!"

He drew out his pipe and turned beaming to the glowering Deering.

"There, my boy! Babette is one of us--one of the great company of the stars! Wonderful, how you find them at every turn! Babette, my sister, I salute you!"

She smiled and turned toward Deering.

"Are you, too, one of the Comrades of Perpetual Youth?" she inquired gravely.

"I am," Deering declared heartily, and they smiled at each other; "but I'm only a novice--a brother of the second class."

She shook her head.

"There can be no question of classes in the great comradeship--either we are or we are not."

"Well spoken!" Hood assented, pushing back his chair and crossing his legs comfortably.

"And you--do you and Pierrette think about things the same way?" Deering asked.

"We do--by not thinking," Babette replied. "Thinking among the comrades is forbidden, is it not?"

"Absolutely," Hood affirmed. "Our young brother here is still a little weak in the faith, but he's taking to it splendidly."

"I'm new myself," Babette confessed.

"You're letter-perfect in the part," said Hood. "Perhaps you were driven to it?

Don't answer if you would be embarrassed by a confession."

The girl pondered a moment; her face grew grave, and she played nervously with the sugar-tongs.

"A man loved me and I sent him away, and was sorry!" The last words fell from her lips falteringly.

"He will come back--if he is worthy of one of the comradeship," said Hood consolingly. "Even now he may be searching for you."

"I was unkind to him; I was very hard on him! And I've been afraid--some-times--that I should never see him again."

Deering thought he saw a glint of tears in her eyes. She rose hastily and asked with a wavering smile:

"If there's nothing further----"

"Not food--if you mean that," said Hood.

"But about Pierrette!" Deering exclaimed despairingly. "If she's likely to come, we must wait for her."

"I rather advise you against it," the girl answered. "I have no idea when she will come back."

They rose instinctively as she passed out. The door fanned a moment and was still.

"Well?" demanded Deering ironically.

"Please don't speak to me in that tone," responded Hood. "This was your break-fast, not mine; you needn't scold me if it didn't go to suit you! Ah, what have we here!"

He had drawn back a curtain at one end of the dining-room, disclosing a studio beyond. It was evidently a practical workshop and bore traces of recent use. Deer-ing passed him and strode toward an easel that supported a canvas on which the paint was still wet. He cried out in astonishment:

"That's the moon girl--that's the girl I talked to last night--clown clothes and all! She's sitting on the wall there just as I found her."

"A sophisticated brush; no amateur's job," Hood muttered, squinting at the canvas. "Seems to me I've seen that sort of thing somewhere lately--Pantaloon, Harlequin, Columbine, and Clown--latest fad in magazine covers. We're in the stu-dio of a popular illustrator--there's a bunch of proofs on the table, and those things on the floor are from the same hand. Signature in the corner a trifle obscure--Mary B. Taylor."

"She may be Babette," Deering suggested. "Suppose I call her and ask?"

Hood, having become absorbed in a portfolio of pen-and-ink sketches of clowns, harlequins, and columbines, subjects in which the owner of the studio apparently specialized, paid no heed to the suggestion. When Deering returned he was gazing critically at a sketch showing a dozen clowns executing a spirited dance on a garden-wall.

"She's skipped! There isn't a soul on the place," Deering announced dejectedly.

"Not at all surprising; probably gone to join her model, Pierrette. And we'd better clear out before we learn too much; life ceases to be interesting when you begin to find the answers to riddles. Pierrette is probably a friend of the artist, and plays model for the fun of it. The same girl is repeated over and over again in these drawings--from which I argue that Pierrette likes to pose and Babette enjoys painting her. We mustn't let this affect the general illusion. The next turn of the road will doubtless bring us to something that can't be explained so easily."

"If it doesn't bring us to Pierrette--" began Deering.

"Tut! None of that! For all you know it may bring us to something infinitely better. Remember that this is mid-May, and anything may happen before June kindles the crimson ramblers. Let us be off."

Half-way across the living-room Deering stopped suddenly.

"My bag--my suitcase!" he shouted.

A suitcase it was beyond question, placed near the door as though to arrest their attention. Deering pounced upon it eagerly and flung it open.

"It's all right--the stuff's here!" he cried huskily.

He began throwing out the packets that filled the case, glancing hurriedly at the seals. Hood lounged near, watching him languidly.

"Most unfortunate," he remarked, noting the growing satisfaction on Deering's face as he continued his examination. "Now that you've found that rubbish, I suppose there'll be no holding you; you'll go back to listen to the ticker just when I had begun to have some hope of you!"

"It was Pierrette that took it; it couldn't have been this artist girl," said Deering, excitedly whipping out his penknife and slitting one of the packages. A sheaf of blank wrapping-paper fluttered to the floor. His face whitened and he gave a cry of dismay. "Robbed! Tricked!" he groaned, staring at Hood.

Hood picked up the paper and scrutinized the seal.

"S. J. Deering, personal," he read in the wax. "You don't suppose that girl has taken the trouble to forge your father's private seal, do you?"

Deering feverishly tore open the other packages.

"All alike; the stuff's gone!"

Perspiration beaded his forehead. He stared stupidly at the worthless paper.

"You ought to be grateful, son," said Hood; "yesterday you thought yourself a thief--now that load's off your mind, and you know yourself for an honest man. General rejoicing seems to be in order. Looks as though your parent had robbed himself--rather a piquant situation, I must say."

He carried the wrappers to the window-seat and examined them more closely.

"Seals were all intact. 'The Tyringham estate,'" he read musingly. "What do you make of that?" he asked Deering, who remained crumpled on the floor beside the suitcase.

"That's an estate father was executor of--it's a long story. Old man Tyringham had been a customer of his, and left a will that made it impossible to close the estate till his son had reached a certain age. The final settlement was to be made this summer. But my God, Hood, do you suppose father--my father could be----"

"A defaulter?" Hood supplied blandly.

"It's impossible!" roared Deering. "Father's the very soul of honor."

"I dare say he is," remarked Hood carelessly. "So were you till greed led you to pilfer your governor's strong box. Let us be tolerant and withhold judgment. It's enough that your own skirts are clear. Put that stuff out of sight; we must flit."

Hood set off for the Barton Arms at a brisk pace, talking incessantly.

"This whole business is bully beyond my highest expectations. By George, it's almost too good to be true! Critics of the drama complain that the average amateur's play ends with every act; but so far in our adventures every incident leads on to something else. Perfectly immense that somebody had beaten you to the bonds!"

Deering's emotions were beyond utterance. It was a warm morning, and he did not relish carrying the suitcase, whose recovery had plunged him into a despair darker than that caused by its loss.

At a turn in the road Hood paused, struck his stick heavily upon the ground, and drew out the slipper. He whirled it in the air three times and twice it pointed east. He thrust it back into his pocket with a sigh of satisfaction and brushed the dust from his hands.

"Once more we shall follow the pointing slipper. Yesterday it led us to the moon girl, the bungalow, and the suitcase; now it points toward the mysterious east, and no telling what new delights!"

VI

Hood and Deering found Cassowary sitting in the machine in the inn yard reading a newspaper; this Hood promptly seized and scanned with his trained eye.

"Are the bags aboard? Ah, I see you have been forehanded, Cassowary!"

Deering went to the inn office and came out with a number of telegrams which he read as he slowly crossed the yard.

"What do you think of this?" he asked weakly. The yellow sheets shook in his hand and his face was white. "I wired to a bank and a club in San Francisco last night, and they've answered that father isn't in San Francisco and hasn't been there! And I wired the people Constance was to visit at Pasadena, and they don't know anything about her. Just look at these things!"

"Sounds like straight information, but why worry?" remarked Hood, scanning the telegrams.

"But why should father lie to me? Why should Constance say she was going to California if she wasn't?"

"My dear boy, don't ask me such questions!" Hood remarked with an injured air. "You are guilty of the gravest error in sending telegrams without consulting me! How can we trust ourselves to Providence if you persist in sending telegrams! If you do this again, I shall be seriously displeased, and you mustn't displease Hood. Hood is very ugly in his wrath."

Deering was at the point of tears. Hood was a fool, and he wished to tell him so, but the words stuck in his throat.

"We move eastward toward the Connecticut border, Cassowary," Hood ordered and pushed Deering into the machine.

Hood was as merry as the morning itself, and talked ceaselessly as they rolled through the country, occasionally bidding Cassowary slow down and give heed to his discourse. The chauffeur listened with a grin, glancing guardedly at Deering, who stared grimly ahead with an unlighted cigar in his mouth. He was not to be disturbed in his meditations upon the blackness of the world by the idiotic prattle of a madman. For half an hour Hood had been describing his adventures with a Dublin University man, whose humor he pronounced the keenest and most satisfying he had ever known. He had gathered from this person an immense fund of lore relating to Irish superstitions.

"He left me just when I had learned to love him," Hood concluded mournfully. "Became fascinated with a patent-medicine faker we struck at a county fair in Indiana. He was so tickled over the way the long-haired doctor played the banjo and jollied the crowd that he attached himself to his caravan. That Irishman was one of the most agreeable men to be in jail with that I ever knew; even hardened murderers would cotton to him. That spire over there must be Addington. The inn is nothing to boast of, but we'd better tackle it."

His gayety at luncheon once more won Deering to a cheerier view of his destiny. Hood called for the proprietor and lectured him roundly for offering canned-blueberry pie. The fact that blueberries were out of season made no difference to the outraged Hood; pie produced from a can was a gross imposition. He cited legal decisions covering such cases and intimated that he might bring proceedings. As the innkeeper strode angrily away an elderly woman at a neighboring table addressed the dining-room on the miserable incompetence of the pastry-cooks of these later times, winding up by thanking Hood heartily for his protest. She was from Boston, she announced, and the declining intellectual life of that city she attributed to the deterioration of its pie.

Hood rose and gravely replied in a speech of five minutes, much to the delight of two girls at the old lady's table. Hood wrote his name on the menu card, and bade the giggling waitress hand it to the lady from Boston. Her young companions conferred for a moment, and then sent back a card on which appeared these names neatly pencilled:

Maid Marian The Queen of Sheba The Duchess of Suffolk (Mass.)

"My dear boy," Hood remarked to Deering after he had bowed elaborately to the trio, "I tell you the whole world's caught step with us! That lady and her two nieces, or granddaughters as the case may be, are under the spell, just as you and I are and Cassowary and your Pierrette and Babette of the bungalow. If only you could yield yourself to the May spirit, how happy we might be! Just think of Cassowary; worth a million dollars and eating his lunch with the chauffeurs somewhere below stairs and picking up much information that he will impart to me later! What a bully world this would be if all mankind followed my system: stupid conventions all broken-down; the god of mirth holding his sides as he contemplates the world at play! You may be sure that old lady is a stickler for the proprieties when she's at home; widow of a bishop most likely. Those girls have been carefully reared, you can see that, but full of the spirit of mischief. The moment I tackled that stupid innkeeper about his monstrous pie they felt the drawing of the mystic tie that binds us together with silken cords. Very likely they, like us, are in search of adventure, and if our own affairs were less urgent I should certainly cultivate their further acquaintance."

The lady who called herself the Duchess of Suffolk (Mass.) was undoubtedly a person of consequence and the possessor of a delightful humor. Deering assumed that she and her companions were abroad upon a lark of some kind and were enjoying themselves tremendously. Hood's spell renewed its grip upon him. It occurred to him that the whole world might have been touched with the May madness, and that the old order of things had passed forever. It seemed ages since he had watched the ticker in his father's office. As they sat smoking on the veranda the Duchess of Suffolk, the Queen of Sheba, and Maid Marian came out and entered a big car. The old lady bowed with dignity as the car moved off; the girls waved their hands.

"Perfect!" Hood muttered as he returned their salutations. "We may never meet again in this world, but the memory of this encounter will abide with me forever."

"I don't want to appear fussy, Hood," Deering began good-naturedly, "but would you mind telling me what's next on your programme?"

"Not in the slightest. It's just occurred to me that it would be well to dine tonight in one of the handsome villas scattered through these hills. Still following the slipper, we shall choose one somewhere east of the inn and present ourselves confidently at the front door. Failing there, we shall assault the postern and, perhaps, enrich our knowledge of life with the servants' gossip."

"There are some famous kennels in this neighborhood, and I'd hate awfully to have an Airedale bite a hole in my leg," Deering suggested.

"My dear boy, that's the tamest thing that could happen to us! My calves are covered with scars from dogs' teeth; you soon get hardened to canine ferocity. We'll take a tramp for an hour to work the fuzz off our gray matter, and then a nap to freshen us up for the evening. We shall learn much to-night; I'm confident of that."

There seemed to be no way of escaping Hood or changing his mind once he announced a decision. The programme was put through exactly as he had indicated. The important thing about the tramp was that Cassowary accompanied them on the walk, and Deering found him both agreeable and interesting. He discoursed of polo, last year's Harvard-Yale football game, and ice-boating, in which he seemed deeply experienced.

Hood left them to look for hieroglyphics on a barn which he said was a veritable palimpsest of cryptic notations of roving thieves.

Cassowary's manner underwent a marked change when he and Deering were alone.

"If you're going to give the old boy the slip," he said earnestly, "I want you to give me notice. I'm not going to be left alone with him."

Their eyes met in a long scrutiny; then Deering laughed.

"I don't know how you feel about it, but, by George, I'm afraid to shake him!"

"That's exactly my fix," Cassowary answered. "I was in a bad way when he picked me up: just about ready to jump off a high building and let it go at that. And I must say he does make things seem brighter. He mustn't see us talking off key, as he'd say, but I'd like to ask you this: what's he running away from? That's what worries me. What's he grabbing newspapers for all the time and slashing out ads and other queer stuff?"

"You've got me there," Deering replied soberly. "We ran into some men the other night who he said were detectives looking for him, but it didn't seem to worry him any."

"There's nothing new in *that*. We've struck a number of men who apparently were looking for somebody, and he greatly enjoys chaffing them. If he's really a crook, he wouldn't be exposing himself to arrest as he does."

Hood was now returning from his investigations of the barn, and as he crossed the pasture was examining a bunch of the newspaper clippings with which his pockets were stuffed.

"You needn't be afraid of getting into trouble with him," Cassowary remarked admiringly. "He pulls off things you wouldn't think could be done. He's a marvel, that man!"

"Old Bill Fogarty's been ripping into the country stores in these parts," began Hood volubly; "found his mark on the barn, all right. Amusing cuss, Fogarty. Sawed himself out of most of the jails between here and Bangor. We'll probably meet up with him somewhere. It's about time to go back for that snooze, boys. To the road again!"

He strode off singing, in a very good tenor voice, snatches from Italian operas, and his pace was so rapid that his companions were hard pressed to keep up with him.

VII

Evening dress was becoming to Hood, enhancing the distinction which his rough corduroys never wholly obscured. He surveyed Deering critically, gave a twist to his tie, and said it was time to be off. As they drove slowly through the country he discussed the various houses they passed, speculating as to the entertainment they offered. He finally ordered Cassowary to stop at the entrance to an imposing estate, where a large colonial mansion stood some distance from the highway.

"This strikes me as promising," he remarked, rising in the car and craning his neck to gain a view of the house through the shrubbery. "Drive in, Cassowary, and stand by with the car till you see whether we have to run for it."

He gave the electric annunciator a prolonged push, and as a butler opened the door advanced into the hall with his most authoritative air.

"Mr. Hood and Mr. Tuck. I trust I correctly understood that we dine at seven." The man eyed them with surprise but took their coats and hats. "We are expected. Please announce us immediately."

Deering followed him bewilderedly into the drawing-room and planted himself close to the door.

"Assurance, my dear boy, conquers all things," Hood declaimed. "This stuff looks like real Chippendale, and the rugs seem to be genuine." He sniffed contemptuously as he posed before a long mirror for a final inspection of his raiment. "It always pains me to detect the odor of boiled vegetables when I enter a strange house. Architects tell me that it is almost impossible to prevent----"

A woman's figure flashed in the mirror beside him, and he whirled round and bowed from the hips.

"I trust you are not so lacking in the sense of hospitality that you find yourself considering means of ejecting us. My comrade and I are weary from a long journey."

Turning quickly, her gaze fell upon Deering, who was stealing on tiptoe toward the door.

"Halt!" commanded Hood.

Deering paused and sheepishly faced his hostess.

She was a small, trim, graceful woman, of the type that greets middle life smilingly and with no fear of what may lie beyond. Her dark hair had whitened, but her rosy cheeks belied its insinuations. She viewed Deering with frank curiosity, but with no indication of alarm. She was not a woman one would consciously annoy, and Deering's face burned as he felt her eyes inspecting him from head to foot. He had never before been so heartily ashamed of himself; once out of this scrape, he meant to escape from Hood and lead a circumspect, orderly life.

"Which is Hood and which is Tuck?" the woman asked with a faint smile.

"The friar is the gentleman standing on one foot at your right," Hood answered. "Conscious of my unworthiness, I plead guilty to being Hood--Hood the hobo delectable, the tramp incomprehensible!"

"Incomprehensible," she repeated; "you strike me as altogether obvious."

"You never made a greater mistake," Hood returned with asperity. "But the question that now agitates us is simply this: do we eat or do we not?"

Deering looked longingly at a chair with which he felt strongly impelled to brain his suave, unruffled companion. Hood apparently was hardened to such encounters, and stood his ground unflinchingly. All Deering's instincts of chivalry were roused by the little woman, who had every reason for turning them out of doors. He resolved to make it easy for her to do so.

"I beg your pardon--" he faltered.

Hood signalled to him furiously behind her back to maintain silence.

"No apology would be adequate," she remarked with dignity. "We'd better drop that and consider your errand on its strict merits."

"Admirably said, madam," Hood rejoined readily. "We ask nothing of you but seats at your table and the favor of a little wholesome and stimulating conversation, which I refuse to believe you capable of denying us."

A clock somewhere began to boom seven. She waited for the last stroke to die away.

"I make it a rule never to deny food to any applicant, no matter how unworthy. You may remain."

Deering had hardly adjusted himself to this when an old gentleman entered the room, and with only the most casual glance at the two pilgrims walked to the grand piano, shook back his cuffs, and began playing Mendelssohn's "Spring Song," as though that particular melody were the one great passion of his life. When he had concluded he rose and shook down his cuffs.

"If that isn't music," he demanded, walking up to the amazed Deering, who still clung to his post by the door, "what is it? Answer me that!"

"You played it perfectly," Deering stammered.

"And you," he demanded, whirling upon Hood, "what have you to say, sir?"

"The great master himself would have envied your touch," Hood replied.

The old gentleman glared. "Rot!" he ejaculated; and then, turning to the mistress of the house, he asked: "Do these ruffians dine with us?"

"They seem about to do us that honor. My father, Mr. Hood, and--Mr. Tuck. Shall we go out to dinner?"

The gentleman she had introduced as her father glared again--a separate glare for each--and, advancing with a ridiculous strut, gave the lady his arm.

In the hall Hood intercepted Deering in the act of effecting egress by way of the front door. His fingers dug deeply into his nervous companion's arm as he dragged him along, talking in his characteristic vein:

"My dear Tuck, it's a pleasure to find ourselves at last in a home whose appointments speak for breeding and taste. The portrait on our right bears all the marks of a genuine Copley. Madam, may I inquire whether I correctly attribute that portrait to our great American master?"

"You are quite right," she answered over her shoulder. "The subject of the portrait is my great-great-grandfather."

"My dear Tuck!" cried Hood jubilantly, still clutching Deering's arm, "fate has again been kind to us; we are among folk of quality, as I had already guessed."

The dining-room was in dark oak; the glow from concealed burners shed a soft light upon a round table.

"You will sit at my right, Mr. Hood, and Mr. Tuck by my father on the other side."

Deering pinched himself to make sure he was awake. The next instant the room whirled, and he clutched the back of his chair for support. A girl came into the room and walked quickly to the seat beside him.

"Mr Hood and Mr. Tuck, my daughter----"

She hesitated, and the girl laughingly ejaculated: "Pierrette!"

"Sit down, won't you, please," said the little lady; but Deering stood staring open-mouthed at the girl.

Beyond question, she was the girl of the Little Dipper; there was no mistaking her. At this point the old gentleman afforded diversion by rising and bowing first to Hood and then to Deering.

"I am Pantaloon," he said. "My daughter is Columbine, as you may have guessed."

"It's very nice to see you again," Pierrette remarked to Deering; "but, of course, I didn't know you would be here. How goes the burgling?"

"I--er--haven't got started yet. I find it a little difficult----"

"I'm afraid you're not getting much fun out of the adventurous life," she suggested, noting the wild look in his eyes.

"I don't understand things, that's all," he confessed, "but I think I'm going to like it."

"You find it a little too full of surprises? Oh, we all do at first! You see grandfather is seventy, and he never grew up, and mamma is just like him. And I--" She shrugged her shoulders and flashed a smile at her grandparent.

"You are wonderful--bewildering," Deering stammered.

The old gentleman was inveighing at Hood upon America's lack of mirth; the American people had utterly lost their capacity for laughter, the old man averred. Deering's fork beat a lively tattoo on his plate as he attacked his caviar.

And then another girl entered and walked to the remaining vacant place opposite him.

"Smeraldina," murmured the mistress of the house, glancing round the table, and calmly finishing a remark the girl's entrance had interrupted.

Deering's last hold upon sanity slowly relaxed. Unless his wits were entirely gone, he was facing his sister Constance. She wore a dark gown, with white collar and cuffs, and her manner was marked by the restraint of an upper servant of some sort who sits at the family table by sufferance. He was about to gasp out her name when she met his eyes with a glinty stare and a quick shake of the head. Then Pierrette addressed a remark to her--kindly meant to relieve her embarrassment-- referring to a walk over the hills they had taken together that afternoon.

"Ah, Smeraldina!" cried Pantaloon, "how is that last chapter? Columbine re- fuses to show me any more of the book until it is finished. I look to you to make a duplicate for my private perusal."

Here was light of a sort upon the strange household; its mistress was a writer of books; Constance was her secretary; but the effort to explain how his sister came to be masquerading in such a role left him doddering, and that she should refuse to recognize him--her own brother!

"If that new book is half as good as 'The Madness of May,'" Pantaloon was say- ing, "I shall not be disappointed."

"Oh, it's much better; infinitely better!" Constance declared warmly.

"Tuck, do you realize we are in the presence of greatness?" cried Hood. Then, turning to Columbine: "The author will please accept my heartiest congratulations!"

"Thank you kindly," replied the hostess. "I'm fortunate in my secretary. Smer- aldina is my fifth, and the first who ever made a suggestion that was of the slightest use. The others had no imagination; they all objected to being called Smeraldina, and one of them was named Smith!"

"I'm afraid I'm the first who ever had the impertinence to suggest anything," Constance answered humbly.

This was not the sister Deering had known in his old life before he fell victim to the prevailing May madness. She was in servitude and evidently trying to make the best of it. She had been the jolliest, the most high-spirited of girls, and to find her now meekly acting as amanuensis to a lady whose very name he didn't know sent his imagination stumbling through the blindest of dark alleys.

Only the near presence of Pierrette and her perfect composure and good-na- ture checked his inclination to stand up and shout to relieve his feelings.

"I hope you don't mind my not turning up for breakfast," she remarked in her low, bell-like tones.

Deering's hopes rose. That breakfast at the bungalow seemed the one tangible incident of his twenty-four hours in Hood's company and, perhaps, if he let her take the lead, he might find himself on solid earth again.

"I'd been week-ending with Babette; she's an artist, you know, and I'm posing for another of mamma's heroines. Babette got me up at daylight to pose for the last picture and then--I skipped and left her to manage the breakfast."

Her laugh as she said this established her identity beyond question. For a moment the thought of the packages of worthless wrapping-paper he had found in his suitcase chilled his happiness in finding her again; but it had not been her fault; the unbroken seals fully established her innocence.

"You understand, of course, that it's a dark secret that mother writes. She had scribbled for her own amusement all her life, and published 'The Madness of May' just to see what the public would do to it."

"I understand that it's immensely amusing," remarked Deering, thrilling as she turned toward him.

"Oh, you haven't read it!" she cried. "Mamma, Mr. Tuck hasn't read your book."

"My young friend is just beginning his education," interposed Hood. "I unhesitatingly pronounce 'The Madness of May' a classic--something the tired world has been awaiting for years!"

"Right!" cried Pantaloon. "You are quite right, sir. 'The Madness of May' isn't a novel, it's a text-book on happiness!"

"Truer words were never spoken!" exclaimed Hood with enthusiasm.

"Do you know," began Deering, when it was possible to address Pierrette directly again, "I don't believe I was built for this life. I find myself checking off the alphabet on my fingers every few minutes to see if I have gone plumb mad!"

She bent toward him with entreaty in her eyes. He observed that they were brown eyes! In the starlight he had been unable to judge of their color, and he was chagrined that he hadn't guessed at that first interview that she was a brown-eyed girl. Only a brown-eyed girl would have hung a moon in a tree! Brown eyes are immensely eloquent of all manner of pleasant things--such as mischief, mirth, and dreams. Moreover, brown eyes are so highly sensitized that they receive and transmit messages in the most secret of ciphers, and yet always with circumspection. He was perfectly satisfied with Pierrette's eyes and relieved that they were not blue, for blue eyes may be cold, and the finest of black eyes are sometimes dull. Gray eyes alone--misty, fathomless gray eyes--share imagination with brown ones. But neither a blue-eyed nor a black-eyed nor a gray-eyed Pierrette was to be thought of. Pierrette's eyes were brown, as he should have known, and what she was saying to him was just what he should have expected once the color of her eyes had been determined.

"Please don't! You must never try to **understand** things like this! You see grandpa and mamma love larking, and this is a lark. We're always larking, you know."

Hood's voice rose commandingly:

"Once when I was in jail in Utica----"

Deering regretted his shortness of leg that made it impossible to kick his erratic companion under the table. But a chorus of approval greeted this promising opening, and Hood continued relating with much detail the manner in which he had once been incarcerated in company with a pickpocket whose accomplishments and engaging personality he described with gusto. There was no denying that Hood talked well, and the strict attention he was receiving evoked his best efforts.

Deering, covertly glancing at his sister, found that she too hung upon Hood's words. Her presence in the house still presented an enigma with which his imagination struggled futilely, but no opportunity seemed likely to offer for an exchange of confidences.

Constance was a thoroughbred and played her part flawlessly. Her treatment by her employer left nothing to be desired; the amusing little grandfather appealed to her now and then with unmistakable liking, and the smiles that passed between her and Pierrette were evidence of the friendliest relationship.

The dinner was served in a leisurely fashion that encouraged talk, and Deering availed himself of every chance for a tete-a-tete with Pierrette. She graciously came down out of the clouds and conversed of things that were within his comprehension--of golf and polo for example--and then passed into the unknown again. But in no way did she so much as hint at her identity. When she referred to her mother or grandfather she employed the pseudonyms by which he already knew them. While they were on the subject of polo he asked her if she had witnessed a certain match.

"Oh, yes, I was there!" she replied. "And, of course, I saw you; you were the star performer. At tea afterward I saw you again, surrounded by admirers." She laughed at his befuddlement. "But it's against all the rules to try to unmask me! Of course, I know you, but maybe you will never know me!"

"I don't believe you are cruel enough to prolong my agony forever! I can't stand this much longer!"

"Perhaps some day," she answered quietly and meeting his eager gaze steadily, "we shall meet just as the people of the world meet, and then maybe you won't like me at all!"

"After this the world will never be the same planet again. Hereafter my business will be to follow you----"

She broke in laughingly, "even to the Little Dipper?"

"Even to the farthest star!" he answered.

After coffee had been served in the drawing-room, Hood, again dominating the company (much to Deering's disgust), suggested music. Pierrette contributed a flashing, golden Chopin waltz and Pantaloon Schubert's "Serenade," which he played atrociously, whereupon Hood announced that he would sing a Scotch ballad, which he proceeded to do surprisingly well. The evening could not last forever, and Deering chafed at his inability to detach Pierrette from the piano; but she was most provokingly submissive to Hood's demand that the music continue. Deering had protested that he didn't sing; he hated himself for not singing!

He fidgeted awhile; then, finding the others fully preoccupied with their musical experiments, quietly left the drawing-room. It had occurred to him that Constance, who had disappeared when they left the table, might be seeking a chance to speak to him and he strolled through the library (a large room with books crowding to the ceiling) to a glass door opening into a conservatory, which was dark save for the light from the library. He was about to turn away when an outer door opened furtively and Cassowary stepped in from the grounds. The chauffeur glanced about nervously as though anxious to avoid detection.

As Deering watched him a shadow darted by, and his sister--unmistakably Constance in the dark gown with its white collar and cuffs that she had worn at dinner--moved swiftly toward the chauffeur. She gave him both hands; he kissed her eagerly; then they began talking earnestly. For several minutes Deering heard the blurred murmur of rapid question and reply; then, evidently disturbed by an outburst of merriment from the drawing-room, the two parted with another handclasp and kiss, and Cassowary darted through the outer door.

Constance waited a moment, as though to compose herself, and then began retracing her steps down the conservatory aisle. As she passed his hiding-place Deering stepped out and seized her arm.

"So this is what's in the wind, is it?" he demanded roughly. "I suppose you don't know that that man's a bad lot, a worthless fellow Hood picked up in the hope of reforming him! For all I know he may be the chauffeur he pretends to be!"

She freed herself and her eyes flashed angrily.

"You don't know what you're saying! That man is a gentleman, and if he went to pieces for a while it was my fault. I met him at the Drakes' last year when you were away hunting in Canada. He came to our house afterward, but for some reason father took one of his strong dislikes to him, and forbade my seeing him again. I knew he was with this man Hood, and when I left the table awhile ago I met him outside the servants' dining-room and told him I would talk to him here."

"What does he call himself?" Deering asked.

"Torrence is the name the Drakes gave him," she answered with faint irony. "He's a ranchman in Wyoming and was in Bob Drake's class in college."

He knew perfectly well that the Drakes were not people likely to countenance an impostor. His first instinct had been to protect his sister from an unknown scamp, and he was sorry that he had spoken to her so roughly. Her distress and anxiety were apparent, and he was filled with pity for her. Since childhood they had been the best of pals, and if she loved a man who was worthy of her he would aid the affair in every way possible. He was surprised by the abruptness with which she stepped close to him and laid her hand on his arm.

"Billy, who *is* Hood?" she whispered.

"I don't know!" he ejaculated, and then as she eyed him curiously he explained hurriedly: "I was in an awful mess when he turned up, Connie. I'd gone into a copper deal with Ned Ranscomb and needed more money to help him through with it. I put in all I had and touched one of father's boxes at the bank for some more and lost it, or didn't lose it; God knows what did become of it! It would take a week to tell you the whole story. Ranscomb disappeared, absolutely, and there I was! I should have killed myself if that lunatic Hood hadn't turned up and hypnotized me. But what--what--" (he fairly choked with the question), "in heaven's name are you doing here? Why did you cut out California? I tell you, Connie, if I'm not crazy everybody else is! I nearly fainted when you came into the dining-room."

Constance smiled at his despair, but hurried on with explanations:

"We can't talk here, but I can clear up a few things. Father read that woman's book, and it went to his head. Yes," she added as Deering groaned in his helplessness, "father's acting a good deal like those people in the drawing-room. He's got the May madness, and I'm afraid I've got a touch of it myself! Father started off to have adventures like the people in that book and dragged me along to get my mind off Tommy----"

"Tommy?"

"Mr. Torrence!"

Billy swallowed this with a gulp.

"But, Billy," Constance continued seriously, "there's really something on father's mind; he thinks he's looking for somebody, and I'm not sure whether he is or not. That's how I come to be here. He made me answer an advertisement and take this position to spy on these people."

"My God!" Deering gasped, "gone clean mad, the whole bunch of us. Who the deuce are these lunatics anyhow?"

"I don't know, Billy; honestly I don't! You know nearly as much about them as I do. Their mail goes to a bank in town, and I met my employer at a lawyer's office in Hartford. Father suspects something and made me do it, so I might watch them. The mother and daughter have been abroad a great deal, and just came home a month ago. I never saw this man Hood until to-night. The mother and daughter and the old gentleman call each other by the names you heard at the table, and the books in the library are marked with half a dozen names. Even the silver gives no clew. I've been here a week and only one person has come to the house" (she lowered her voice to a whisper), "and that was Ned Ranscomb!"

He clutched her hands, and the words he tried to utter became a queer, inarticulate gurgle in his throat.

"Ned came here to see a girl," she went on: "an artist who made the pictures for 'The Madness of May.' He's quite crazy about her. I did get that much out of Pierrette. This artist's a victim of the madness too, and seems to be leading Ned a gay dance!"

"Took my two hundred thousand and got me to steal two more," he groaned, "and then went chasing a girl all over creation! And the fool always bragged that he was immune; that no girl----"

"Another victim of the same disease, that's all," answered Constance with a wry smile.

"Not Ned; not Ranscomb! That settles it! We've all gone loony!"

"Well, even so, we mustn't be caught here," said Constance with decision as the music ceased.

"Tell me, quick, where can I find the governor?" Deering demanded.

"If you *must* know, Billy," she replied, her lips quivering with mirth, "our dear parent is in jail--in *jail*! Tommy collected those glad tidings at the garage."

Having launched this at her astounded brother, she pushed him from her and ran away through the conservatory.

VIII

T uck, my boy, you should cultivate the art of music!" cried Hood as Deering reappeared, somewhat pale but resigned to an unknown fate, in the drawing-room. "And now that ten has struck we must be on our way. Madam, will you ring for Cassowary, the prince of chauffeurs, as we must leave your hospitable home at once?" He began making his adieus with the greatest formality.

"Mr. Tuck," said the mistress of the house as Deering gave her a limp hand, "you have conferred the greatest honor upon us. Please never pass our door without stopping."

"To-morrow," he said, turning to Pierrette, "I shall find you to-morrow, either here or in the Dipper!"

"Before you see me or the Dipper again, many things may happen!" she laughed.

The trio--the absurd little Pantaloon; Columbine, laughing and gracious to the last, and Pierrette, smiling, charming, adorable--cheerily called good night from the door as Cassowary sent the car hurrying out of the grounds.

"Well, what do you think of the life of freedom now?" demanded Hood as the car reached the open road. "Begin to have a little faith in me, eh?"

"Well, you seemed to put it over," Deering admitted grudgingly. "But I can't go on this way, Hood; I really can't stand it. I've got to quit right now!"

"My dear boy!" Hood protested.

"I've heard bad news about my father; one of the--er--servants back there told me he was in jail!"

"Stop!" bawled Hood. "This is important if true! Cassowary, I've told you time and again to bring me any news you pick up in servants' halls. What have you heard about the arrest of a gentleman named Deering?"

"He's been pinched, all right," the chauffeur answered as he stopped the car and turned round. "The constables over at West Dempster are trapping joy-riders, and they nailed Mr. Deering about sundown for speeding. I learned that from the chauffeur at that house where you dined."

Hood slapped his knee and chortled with delight.

"There's work ahead of us! But probably he's bailed himself out by this time."

"Not on your life!" Cassowary answered, and Deering marked a note of jubilation in his tone, as though the thought of Mr. Deering's incarceration gave him pleasure. "The magistrate's away for the night, and there's nobody there to fix bail. It's part of the treatment in these parts to hold speed fiends a night or two."

Again Hood's hand fell upon Deering's knee.

"A situation to delight the gods!" he cried. "Cassowary, old man, at the next crossroads turn to the right and run in at the first gate. There's a farmhouse in the midst of an orchard; we'll stop there and change our clothes."

As the car started Deering whirled upon Hood and shook him violently by the collar.

"I'm sick of all this rot! I can't stand any more, I tell you. I'm going to quit right here!"

Hood drew his arm round him affectionately.

"My dear son, have I failed you at any point? Have you ever in your life had any adventures to compare with those you've had with me? Stop whining and trust all to Hood!"

Deering sank back into his corner with a growl of suppressed rage.

When they reached the farmhouse Hood drew out a key and opened the front door with a proprietorial air.

"Whose place is this? I want to know what I'm getting in for," Deering demanded wrathfully.

"Mine, dearest Tuck! Mine, and the taxes paid. I use it as a rest-house for weary and jaded crooks, if that will ease your mind!"

Cassowary struck matches and lighted candles, disclosing a half-furnished room in great disorder. Old clothing, paper bags that had contained food, a violin, and books in good bindings littered a table in the middle of the floor, and articles of clothing were heaped in confusion on a time-battered settle. The odor of stale pipe smoke hung upon the air. Under an empty bottle on the mantel Hood found a scrap of paper which he scanned for a moment and then tore into pieces.

"Just a scratch from good old Fogarty; he's been taking the rest-cure here between jobs. Skipped yesterday; same chap that left his mark for me on that barn. One of the royal good fellows, Fogarty; does his work neatly--never carries a gun or pots a cop; knows he can climb out of any jail that ever was made, and that, son, gives any man a joyful sense of ease and security. The Tombs might hold him, but he avoids large cities; knows his limitations like a true man of genius. Rare bird; thrifty doesn't describe him; he's just plain stingy; sells stolen postage-stamps at par; the only living yegg that can put that over! By George, I wouldn't be surprised if he couldn't sell 'em at a premium!"

As he talked he rummaged among the old clothes, chose a mud-splashed pair of trousers, and bade Deering put them on, adding an even more disreputable coat and hat. Cassowary helped himself to a change of raiment, and Hood selected what seemed to be the worst of the lot.

"Three suspicious characters will be noted by the constabulary of West Dempster within two hours!" cried Hood, hopping out of his dress trousers. "Into the calaboose we shall go, my dear Tuck! Never say that I haven't a thought for your peace and happiness. It will give me joy unfeigned to bring you face to face with your delightful parent. Cassowary, my son, I'm going to hide those bills of yours in the lining of my coat for safety. If they found ten thousand plunks on me, they'd never let us go!"

"Hood!" cried Deering in a voice moist with tears, "for God's sake what fool thing are you up to now?"

"I tell you we're going to jail!" Hood answered jubilantly. "You've dined in good company with the most charming of girls at your side; you've had a taste of the prosperous life; and now it's fitting that we should touch the other extreme. The moment we step out of this shack we're criminals, crooks, gallows meat;" he rolled this last term under his tongue unctuously. "This will top all our other adventures. Here's hoping Fogarty may have preceded us. The old boy likes to get pinched occasionally just for the fun of it."

He was already blowing out the candles, and, seizing his stick, led the way back to the highway, with Deering and Cassowary at his heels. The car had been run into an old barn, which had evidently served Hood before. Within twenty-four hours they would be touring again, he announced. The change from his dress clothes to ill-fitting rags had evidently wrought a change of mood. Between whiffs at his pipe he sought consolation in Wagner, chanting bars of "In *fernem* Land."

Cassowary, who had adjusted himself to this new situation without question, whispered in Deering's ear: "Don't kick; he's got something up his sleeve. And he'll get you out of it; remember that! I've been in jail with him before."

Deering drew away impatiently. He was in no humor to welcome confidences from Torrence, *alias* Cassowary, whom his sister met clandestinely and *kissed*--the kiss rankled! And yet it was nothing against Cassowary that he had been following Hood about like an infatuated fool. Deering knew himself to be equally culpable on that score, and he was even now trudging after the hypnotic vagabond with a country calaboose as their common goal. The chauffeur's interview with Constance had evidently cheered him mightily, and he joined his voice to Hood's in a very fair rendering of "Ben Bolt." Deering swore under his breath, angry at Hood, and furious that he had so little control of a destiny that seemed urging him on to destruction.

IX

At one o'clock West Dempster lay dark and silent before them. As they crossed a bridge into the town Hood began to move cautiously.

"Remember that we give up without a struggle: there's too much at stake to risk a bullet now, and these country lumpkins shoot first, and hand you their cards afterward."

He dived into an alley, and emerged midway of a block where a number of barrels under a shed awning advertised a grocery.

"Admirable!" whispered Hood, throwing his arms about his comrades. "We will now arouse the watch."

With this he kicked a barrel into the gutter, and jumped back like a mischievous boy into the shelter of the alley. Footsteps were heard in a moment, far down the street.

"These country cops are sometimes shrewd, but often the silly children of convention like the rest of us. West Dempster has an evil reputation in the underworld. The pinching of joy-riders is purely incidental; they run in anybody they catch after the curfew sounds from the coffin factory."

A window overhead opened with a bang, and a blast from a police whistle pierced the air shrilly. Deering started to run, but Hood upset him with a thrust of his foot. Two men were already creeping up behind them in the alley; the owner of the grocery stole out of the front door in a long nightgown and began howling dismally for help.

"Throw up your hands, boys; it's no use!" cried Hood in mock despair.

Then the man in the nightgown, after menacing Hood with a pistol, stuck the barrel of it into Deering's mouth, opened inopportunely to protest his innocence. The policemen threw themselves upon Hood and Cassowary, toppled them over, and flashed electric lamps in their faces.

"More o' them yeggs," announced one of the officers with satisfaction as he snapped a pair of handcuffs on Cassowary's wrists. "Don't you fellows try any monkey-shines or we'll plug you full o' lead. Trot along now."

The gentleman in the night-robe wished to detain the party for a recital of his own prowess in giving warning of the attempted burglary. The police were disposed to make light of his assistance, while Hood hung back to support the grocer's cause, a generosity on his part that was received ill-temperedly by the officers of the law. They bade the grocer report to the magistrate Monday morning, and they parted, but only after Hood had shaken the crestfallen grocer warmly by the hand, warning him with the greatest solicitude against further exposure to the night air. Two other policemen appeared; the whole force was doing them honor, Hood declared proudly. He lifted his voice in song, but the lyrical impulse was hushed by a prod from a revolver. He continued to talk, however, assuring his captors of his heartiest admiration for their efficiency. He meant to recommend them for positions in the secret service--men of their genius were wasted upon a country town.

When they reached the town hall a melancholy jailer roused himself and conducted them to the lockup in the rear of the building. Careful search revealed nothing but a mass of crumpled clippings and a pipe and tobacco in Hood's pockets.

"Guess they dropped their tools somewhere," muttered one of the officers.

"My dear boy," explained Hood, "the gentleman in the nightie, whom I take to be a citizen and merchant of standing in your metropolis, may be able to assist you in finding them. We left our safe-blowing apparatus in a chicken-coop in his back yard."

They were entered on the blotter as R. Hood, F. Tuck, and Cass O'Weary--the last Hood spelled with the utmost care for the scowling turnkey--and charged with attempt to commit burglary and arson.

Hood grumbled; he had hoped it would be murder or piracy on the high seas; burglary and arson were so commonplace, he remarked with a sigh.

The door closed upon them with an echoing clang, and they found themselves in a large coop, bare save for several benches ranged along the walls. Two of these were occupied by prisoners, one of whom, a short, thick-set man, snored vociferously. Hood noted his presence with interest.

"Fogarty!" he whispered with a triumphant wave of his hand.

A tall man who had chosen a cot as remote as possible from his fellow prisoner sat up and, seeing the newcomers, stalked majestically to the door and yelled dismally for the keeper, who lounged indifferently to the cage, puffing a cigar.

"This is an outrage!" roared the prisoner. "Locking me up with these felons-- these common convicts! I demand counsel; I'm going to have a writ of habeas corpus! When I get out of here I'm going to go to the governor of your damned State and complain of this. All Connecticut shall know of it! All America shall hear of it! To be locked up with one safe-blower is enough, and now you've stuck three murderers into this rotten hole. I tell you I can give bail. I tell you----"

The jailer snarled and bade him be quiet. In the tone of a man who is careful of his words he threatened the direst punishment for any further expression of the gentleman's opinions. Whereupon the gentleman seized the bars and shook them violently, and then, as though satisfied that they were steel of the best quality, dropped his arms to his sides with a gesture of impotent despair.

"Father!"

In spite of Constance's assertion, confirmed by Cassowary, Deering had not believed that his father was in jail; but the outraged gentleman who had demanded the writ of habeas corpus was, beyond question, Samuel J. Deering, head of the banking-house of Deering, Gaylord & Co. Mr. Deering was striding toward his bench with the sulky droop of a premium batter who has struck out with the bases full.

Scorning to glance at the creature in rags who had flung himself in his path, Samuel J. Deering lunged at him fiercely with his right arm. Billy, ducking opportunely, saved his indignant parent from tumbling upon the floor by catching him in his arms. Feeling that he had been attacked by a ruffian, Mr. Deering yelled that he was being murdered.

"I'm Billy! For God's sake, be quiet!"

The senior Deering tottered to the wall.

"Billy! What are *you* in for?" he demanded finally.

"Burglary, arson, and little things like that," Billy answered with a jauntiness that surprised him as much as it pained his father, who continued to stare uncomprehendingly.

"You've been reading that damned book, too, have you?" he whispered hoarsely in his son's ear. "You've gone crazy like everybody else, have you?"

"I've been kidnapped, if that's what you mean," Billy answered with a meaningful glance over his shoulder, and then with a fine attempt at bravado: "I'm Friar Tuck, and that chap smoking a pipe is Robin Hood."

Ordinarily his father's sense of humor could be trusted to respond to an intelligent appeal. A slow grin had overspread Mr. Deering's face as Friar Tuck was mentioned, but when Billy added Robin Hood his father's countenance underwent changes indicative of hope, fear, and chagrin. Clinging to Billy's shoulder, he peered through the gloom of the cage toward Hood, who lay on a bench, his coat rolled up for a pillow, tranquilly smoking, with his eyes fixed upon the steel roof.

"Hood!" Mr. Deering walked slowly toward Hood's bench.

Hood sat up, took his pipe from his mouth, and nodded.

"Hood, this is my father," said Billy.

"A great pleasure, I'm sure," Hood responded courteously, extending his hand. "I suppose it was inevitable that we should meet sooner or later, Mr. Deering."

"You--you *are* Bob--Bob--Tyringham?" asked Deering anxiously.

"Right!" cried Hood in his usual assured manner. "And I will say for you that you have given me a good chase. I confess that I didn't think you capable of it; I swear I didn't! Tuck, I congratulate you; your father is one of the true brotherhood of the stars. He's been chasing me for a month and, by Jove, he's kept me guessing! But when I heard that he'd been jailed for speeding, with a prospect of spending Sunday in this hole, I decided that it was time to throw down the mask."

Lights began to dance in the remote recesses of Billy's mind. Hood was Robert Tyringham, for whom his father held as trustee two million dollars. Tyringham had not been heard of in years. The only son of a most practical father, he had been from youth a victim of the *wanderlust*, absenting himself from home for long periods. For ten years he had been on the list of the missing. That Hood should be this man was unbelievable. But the senior Deering seemed not to question his identity. He sat down with a deep sigh and then began to laugh.

"If I hadn't found you by next Wednesday, I should have had to turn your property over to a dozen charitable institutions provided for by your father's will-- and, by George, I've been fighting a temptation to steal it!" His arms clasped Billy's shoulder convulsively. "It's been horrible, ghastly! I've been afraid I might find you and afraid I wouldn't! I tell you it's been hell. I've spent thousands of dollars trying to find you, fearing one day you might turn up, and the next day afraid you wouldn't. And, you know, Tyringham, your father was my dearest friend; that's what made it all so horrible. I want you to know about it, Billy; I want you to know the worst about me; I'm not the man you thought me. When I started away with Constance and told you I was going to California I decided to make a last effort to find Tyringham. I read a damned novel that acted on me like a poison; that's why I've made a fool of myself in a thousand ways, thinking that by masquerading over the country I might catch Tyringham at his own game. And now you know what I might have been; you see what I was trying to be--a common thief, a betrayer of a sacred trust."

"Don't talk like that, father," began Billy, shaken by his father's humility. "I guess we're in the same hole, only I'm in deeper. I tried to rob *you*. I tried to steal some of that Tyringham money myself, but--but----"

Hood, wishing to leave the two alone for their further confidences, walked to the recumbent Fogarty, roused him with a dig in the ribs, and conferred with him in low tones.

"You took the stuff from my box, Billy?" Mr. Deering asked.

Billy waited apprehensively for what might follow. It was possible that his father had already robbed the Tyringham estate; the thought chilled him into dejection.

"I *had* stolen it. My God, I couldn't help it!" Deering groaned. "I left that waste paper in the box to fool myself, and put the real stuff in another place. I hoped--yes, that was it, I hoped--I'd never find Tyringham and I could keep those bonds. But all the time I kept looking for him. You see, Billy, I couldn't be as bad as I wanted to be; and yet----"

He drew his hand across his face as though to shut out the picture he saw of himself as a felon.

"Oh, you wouldn't have done it; you couldn't have done it!" cried Billy, anxious to mitigate his father's misery. "If you hadn't hidden the real bonds, I'd have been a thief! Ned Ranscomb was trying to corner Mizpah and needed my help. I put in all I had--that two hundred thousand you gave me my last birthday, and then he skipped. When I get hold of **him**----!"

"You put two hundred thousand in Mizpah?"

"I did, like a fool, and, of course, it's lost! Ned went daffy about a girl and dropped Mizpah--and my money!"

Mr. Deering was once more a business man. "What did Ranscomb buy at?" he asked curtly.

"Seven and a quarter."

"Then you needn't kick Ned! The Ranscombs put through their deal and Mizpah's gone to forty!"

Hood rejoined them, and they talked till daylight. He told them much of himself. The responsibility of a great fortune had not appealed to him; he had been honest in his preference for the vagabond life, but realized, now that he was well launched upon middle age, that it was only becoming and decent for him to alter his ways. Billy's liking for him, that had struggled so rebelliously against impatience and distrust, warmed to the heartiest admiration.

"Of course I knew you were married," the senior Deering remarked for Billy's enlightenment, "and now and then I got glimpses of you in your gypsy life. Your wife had a fortune of her own--she was one of Augustus Davis's daughters--so of course she hasn't suffered from your foolishness."

"My wife shared my tastes; there has never been the slightest trouble between us. Our daughter is just like us. But now Mrs. Tyringham thinks we ought to settle down and be respectable."

"I knew your wife and daughter had come home. I had got that far," Mr. Deering resumed. "And after I began to suspect that you and Hood were the same person I put my own daughter into your house on the Dempster road as a spy to watch for you."

"My wife wasn't fooled for a minute," Hood chuckled. "We were having our last fling before we settled down for the rest of our days. We all have the same weakness for a springtime lark: my wife, my daughter, and I."

Billy ran his hands through his hair. "Pierrette! Pierrette is your daughter!"

"Certainly," replied Hood; "and Columbine, the dearest woman in the world, is my wife, and Pantaloon my father-in-law. In my affair with you there was only one coincidence: everything else was planned. It was Pierrette, whose real name is Roberta--Bobby for short, when we're not playing a game of some sort--Bobby really did lift your suitcase by mistake. And it was stowed away in Cassowary's car when I came to your house intending to return it. But when I saw that you needed diversion I decided to give you a whirl. It was an easy matter for Cassowary to move the suitcase to the bungalow, where you found it. I steered you to the house on purpose to see how you and Bobby would hit it off. The result seems to have been satisfactory!"

Cassowary turned uneasily on his bench.

"And before we quit all this foolishness," Hood resumed with a glance at the chauffeur, "there's one thing I want to ask you, Mr. Deering, as a special favor. That chap lying over there is Tommy Torrence, whom you kicked off your door-step for daring to love your daughter. He's one of the best fellows in the world. Just because his father, the old senator, didn't quite hit it off with you in a railroad deal before Tommy was born is no reason why you should take it out on the boy. He started for the bad after you made a row over his attentions to your daughter, but he's been with me six months and he's as right and true a chap as ever lived. You've got to fix it up with him or I'll--I'll--well, I'll be pretty hard on your boy if he ever wants to break into my family!"

With this Hood rose and drew from his pocket a handful of newspaper clippings which he threw into the air and watched flutter to the floor.

"Those are some of your advertisements offering handsome rewards for news of me dead or alive. In collecting them I've had a mighty good time. Let's all go to sleep; to-morrow night the genial Fogarty will get us out of this. He's over there now sawing the first bar of that window!"

X

A year has passed and it is May again and the last day of that month of enchantment. There has been a house-party at the Deering place at Radford Hills. Constance came from Wyoming to spend May with her father, bringing with her, of course, her husband, sometime known as Cassowary, who has been elected to the legislature of his State and, may, it is reported, be governor one of these days. The Tyringhams are there, and this includes Robert Tyringham, *alias* R. Hood, and his wife (whose authorship of "The Madness of May," has not yet been acknowledged) and also her father, Augustus Davis, who continues to find recreation in frequent attacks upon any inoffensive piano that gets in his way. Mr. and Mrs. Edward Ranscomb, too, have shared Mr. Deering's hospitality. Marriage has not interrupted Mrs. Ranscomb's career as an artist, though she has dropped illustrating, and is specializing in children's portraits with distinguished success.

The senior Deering, wholly at peace with his conscience, does not work as hard as he used to before his taste of adventurous life gained in the pursuit of Hood. He is very proud of his daughter-in-law, whose brown eyes bring constant cheer and happiness to his table. If she does not hang moons in trees any more, she is still quite capable of doing so, and has no idea of permitting her husband to wear himself out in the banking-house. They are going to keep some time every year for play, she declares, to the very end of their lives.

Hood had been devoting himself assiduously to mastering the details of his business affairs, living as other men do, keeping regular office hours in a tall building with an outlook toward the sea, and taking his recreation on the golf-links every other afternoon.

"Mamma has been nervous all this month about papa," Roberta (known otherwise as Pierrette or Bobby) was saying as she and Billy slowly paced the veranda. "But now May is over and he hasn't shown any disposition to run away. I suppose he's really cured." There was a tinge of regret in her last words.

"Yes," Billy replied carelessly. "He hasn't mentioned his old roving days lately. I think he's even sensitive about having them referred to."

"But even if he should want to go, mamma wouldn't break her heart about it. She feels that it's really something fine in him: his love of the out-of-doors, and adventures, and knowing all sorts and conditions of men. And he has really helped lots of people, just as he helped you. And he always had so much fun when we all played gypsy, or he went off alone and came back with no end of good stories. I'm just a little sorry----"

They paused, clasping hands and looking off at the starry canopy. Suddenly from the side of the house a man walked slowly, hesitatingly. He stopped, turned, glanced at the veranda, and then, sniffing the air, walked rapidly toward the gate, swinging a stick, his face lifted to the stars.

Bobby's hand clasped Billy's more tightly as they watched in silence.

"It's papa; he's taking to the road again!" she murmured.

"But he'll come back; it won't be for long this time. I haven't the heart to stop him!"

"No," she said softly, "it would be cruel to do that."

The lamps at the gate shone upon Robert Tyringham as he paused and then, with a characteristic flourish of his stick, turned westward and strode away into the night.

www.bookjungle.com *email: sales@bookjungle.com fax: 630-214-0564 mail: Book Jungle PO Box 2226 Champaign, IL 61825*

The Codes Of Hammurabi And Moses
W. W. Davies

The discovery of the Hammurabi Code is one of the greatest achievements of archaeology, and is of paramount interest, not only to the student of the Bible, but also to all those interested in ancient history...

Religion   **ISBN:** *1-59462-338-4*

QTY

Pages:132
MSRP $12.95

The Theory of Moral Sentiments
Adam Smith

This work from 1749. contains original theories of conscience amd moral judgment and it is the foundation for systemof morals.

Philosophy **ISBN:** *1-59462-777-0*

QTY

Pages:536
MSRP $19.95

Jessica's First Prayer
Hesba Stretton

In a screened and secluded corner of one of the many railway-bridges which span the streets of London there could be seen a few years ago, from five o'clock every morning until half past eight, a tidily set-out coffee-stall, consisting of a trestle and board, upon which stood two large tin cans, with a small fire of charcoal burning under each so as to keep the coffee boiling during the early hours of the morning when the work-people were thronging into the city on their way to their daily toil...

Childrens   **ISBN:** *1-59462-373-2*

QTY

Pages:84
MSRP $9.95

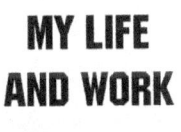

My Life and Work
Henry Ford

Henry Ford revolutionized the world with his implementation of mass production for the Model T automobile. Gain valuable business insight into his life and work with his own auto-biography... "We have only started on our development of our country we have not as yet, with all our talk of wonderful progress, done more than scratch the surface. The progress has been wonderful enough but..."

Biographies/ **ISBN:** *1-59462-198-5*

QTY

Pages:300
MSRP $21.95

www.bookjungle.com *email: sales@bookjungle.com fax: 630-214-0564 mail: Book Jungle PO Box 2226 Champaign, IL 61825*

The Art of Cross-Examination
Francis Wellman

QTY

I presume it is the experience of every author, after his first book is published upon an important subject, to be almost overwhelmed with a wealth of ideas and illustrations which could readily have been included in his book, and which to his own mind, at least, seem to make a second edition inevitable. Such certainly was the case with me; and when the first edition had reached its sixth impression in five months, I rejoiced to learn that it seemed to my publishers that the book had met with a sufficiently favorable reception to justify a second and considerably enlarged edition. ..

Pages:412

Reference   **ISBN:** *1-59462-647-2*   *MSRP $19.95*

On the Duty of Civil Disobedience
Henry David Thoreau

QTY

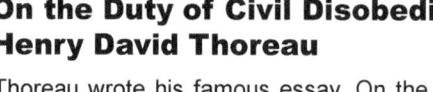

Thoreau wrote his famous essay, On the Duty of Civil Disobedience, as a protest against an unjust but popular war and the immoral but popular institution of slave-owning. He did more than write—he declined to pay his taxes, and was hauled off to gaol in consequence. Who can say how much this refusal of his hastened the end of the war and of slavery ?

Law   **ISBN:** *1-59462-747-9*   **Pages:48**

MSRP $7.45

Dream Psychology Psychoanalysis for Beginners
Sigmund Freud

QTY

Sigmund Freud, born Sigismund Schlomo Freud (May 6, 1856 - September 23, 1939), was a Jewish-Austrian neurologist and psychiatrist who co-founded the psychoanalytic school of psychology. Freud is best known for his theories of the unconscious mind, especially involving the mechanism of repression; his redefinition of sexual desire as mobile and directed towards a wide variety of objects; and his therapeutic techniques, especially his understanding of transference in the therapeutic relationship and the presumed value of dreams as sources of insight into unconscious desires.

Pages:196

Psychology   **ISBN:** *1-59462-905-6*   *MSRP $15.45*

The Miracle of Right Thought
Orison Swett Marden

QTY

Believe with all of your heart that you will do what you were made to do. When the mind has once formed the habit of holding cheerful, happy, prosperous pictures, it will not be easy to form the opposite habit. It does not matter how improbable or how far away this realization may see, or how dark the prospects may be, if we visualize them as best we can, as vividly as possible, hold tenaciously to them and vigorously struggle to attain them, they will gradually become actualized, realized in the life. But a desire, a longing without endeavor, a yearning abandoned or held indifferently will vanish without realization.

Pages:360

Self Help   **ISBN:** *1-59462-644-8*   *MSRP $25.45*

QTY

The Rosicrucian Cosmo-Conception Mystic Christianity *by Max Heindel*   ISBN: *1-59462-188-8*   **$38.95**
The Rosicrucian Cosmo-conception is not dogmatic, neither does it appeal to any other authority than the reason of the student. It is: not controversial, but is: sent forth in the, hope that it may help to clear...   New Age/Religion Pages 646

Abandonment To Divine Providence *by Jean-Pierre de Caussade*   ISBN: *1-59462-228-0*   **$25.95**
"The Rev. Jean Pierre de Caussade was one of the most remarkable spiritual writers of the Society of Jesus in France in the 18th Century. His death took place at Toulouse in 1751. His works have gone through many editions and have been republished...   Inspirational Religion Pages 400

Mental Chemistry *by Charles Haanel*   ISBN: *1-59462-192-6*   **$23.95**
Mental Chemistry allows the change of material conditions by combining and appropriately utilizing the power of the mind. Much like applied chemistry creates something new and unique out of careful combinations of chemicals the mastery of mental chemistry...   New Age Pages 354

The Letters of Robert Browning and Elizabeth Barret Barrett 1845-1846 vol II   ISBN: *1-59462-193-4*   **$35.95**
by Robert Browning and Elizabeth Barrett   Biographies Pages 596

Gleanings In Genesis (volume I) *by Arthur W. Pink*   ISBN: *1-59462-130-6*   **$27.45**
Appropriately has Genesis been termed "the seed plot of the Bible" for in it we have, in germ form, almost all of the great doctrines which are afterwards fully developed in the books of Scripture which follow...   Religion/Inspirational Pages 420

The Master Key *by L. W. de Laurence*   ISBN: *1-59462-001-6*   **$30.95**
In no branch of human knowledge has there been a more lively increase of the spirit of research during the past few years than in the study of Psychology, Concentration and Mental Discipline. The requests for authentic lessons in Thought Control, Mental Discipline and...   New Age/Business Pages 422

The Lesser Key Of Solomon Goetia *by L. W. de Laurence*   ISBN: *1-59462-092-X*   **$9.95**
This translation of the first book of the "Lemegton" which is now for the first time made accessible to students of Talismanic Magic was done, after careful collation and edition, from numerous Ancient Manuscripts in Hebrew, Latin, and French...   New Age/Occult Pages 92

Rubaiyat Of Omar Khayyam *by Edward Fitzgerald*   ISBN:*1-59462-332-5*   **$13.95**
Edward Fitzgerald, whom the world has already learned, in spite of his own efforts to remain within the shadow of anonymity, to look upon as one of the rarest poets of the century, was born at Bredfield, in Suffolk, on the 31st of March, 1809. He was the third son of John Purcell...   Music Pages 172

Ancient Law *by Henry Maine*   ISBN: *1-59462-128-4*   **$29.95**
The chief object of the following pages is to indicate some of the earliest ideas of mankind, as they are reflected in Ancient Law, and to point out the relation of those ideas to modern thought.   Religion/History Pages 452

Far-Away Stories *by William J. Locke*   ISBN: *1-59462-129-2*   **$19.45**
"Good wine needs no bush, but a collection of mixed vintages does. And this book is just such a collection. Some of the stories I do not want to remain buried for ever in the museum files of dead magazine-numbers an author's not unpardonable vanity..."   Fiction Pages 272

Life of David Crockett *by David Crockett*   ISBN: *1-59462-250-7*   **$27.45**
"Colonel David Crockett was one of the most remarkable men of the times in which he lived. Born in humble life, but gifted with a strong will, an indomitable courage, and unremitting perseverance...   Biographies/New Age Pages 424

Lip-Reading *by Edward Nitchie*   ISBN: *1-59462-206-X*   **$25.95**
Edward B. Nitchie, founder of the New York School for the Hard of Hearing, now the Nitchie School of Lip-Reading, Inc, wrote "LIP-READING Principles and Practice". The development and perfecting of this meritorious work on lip-reading was an undertaking...   How-to Pages 400

A Handbook of Suggestive Therapeutics, Applied Hypnotism, Psychic Science   ISBN: *1-59462-214-0*   **$24.95**
by Henry Munro   Health/New Age/Health/Self-help Pages 376

A Doll's House: and Two Other Plays *by Henrik Ibsen*   ISBN: *1-59462-112-8*   **$19.95**
Henrik Ibsen created this classic when in revolutionary 1848 Rome. Introducing some striking concepts in playwriting for the realist genre, this play has been studied the world over.   Fiction/Classics/Plays 308

The Light of Asia *by sir Edwin Arnold*   ISBN: *1-59462-204-3*   **$13.95**
In this poetic masterpiece, Edwin Arnold describes the life and teachings of Buddha. The man who was to become known as Buddha to the world was born as Prince Gautama of India but he rejected the worldly riches and abandoned the reigns of power when... Religion/History/Biographies Pages 170

The Complete Works of Guy de Maupassant *by Guy de Maupassant*   ISBN: *1-59462-157-8*   **$16.95**
"For days and days, nights and nights, I had dreamed of that first kiss which was to consecrate our engagement, and I knew not on what spot I should put my lips..."   Fiction/Classics Pages 240

The Art of Cross-Examination *by Francis L. Wellman*   ISBN: *1-59462-309-0*   **$26.95**
Written by a renowned trial lawyer, Wellman imparts his experience and uses case studies to explain how to use psychology to extract desired information through questioning.   How-to/Science/Reference Pages 408

Answered or Unanswered? *by Louisa Vaughan*   ISBN: *1-59462-248-5*   **$10.95**
Miracles of Faith in China   Religion Pages 112

The Edinburgh Lectures on Mental Science (1909) *by Thomas*   ISBN: *1-59462-008-3*   **$11.95**
This book contains the substance of a course of lectures recently given by the writer in the Queen Street Hall, Edinburgh. Its purpose is to indicate the Natural Principles governing the relation between Mental Action and Material Conditions...   New Age/Psychology Pages 148

Ayesha *by H. Rider Haggard*   ISBN: *1-59462-301-5*   **$24.95**
Verily and indeed it is the unexpected that happens! Probably if there was one person upon the earth from whom the Editor of this, and of a certain previous history, did not expect to hear again...   Classics Pages 380

Ayala's Angel *by Anthony Trollope*   ISBN: *1-59462-352-X*   **$29.95**
The two girls were both pretty, but Lucy who was twenty-one who supposed to be simple and comparatively unattractive, whereas Ayala was credited, as her Bombwhat romantic name might show, with poetic charm and a taste for romance. Ayala when her father died was nineteen...   Fiction Pages 484

The American Commonwealth *by James Bryce*   ISBN: *1-59462-286-8*   **$34.45**
An interpretation of American democratic political theory. It examines political mechanics and society from the perspective of Scotsman James Bryce   Politics Pages 572

Stories of the Pilgrims *by Margaret P. Pumphrey*   ISBN: *1-59462-116-0*   **$17.95**
This book explores pilgrims religious oppression in England as well as their escape to Holland and eventual crossing to America on the Mayflower, and their early days in New England...   History Pages 268

QTY

The Fasting Cure *by Sinclair Upton*   **ISBN:** *1-59462-222-1*   **$13.95**
In the Cosmopolitan Magazine for May, 1910, and in the Contemporary Review (London) for April, 1910, I published an article dealing with my experiences in fasting. I have written a great many magazine articles, but never one which attracted so much attention...   New Age/Self Help/Health Pages 164

Hebrew Astrology *by Sepharial*   **ISBN:** *1-59462-308-2*   **$13.45**
In these days of advanced thinking it is a matter of common observation that we have left many of the old landmarks behind and that we are now pressing forward to greater heights and to a wider horizon than that which represented the mind-content of our progenitors...   Astrology Pages 144

Thought Vibration or The Law of Attraction in the Thought World   **ISBN:** *1-59462-127-6*   **$12.95**
*by **William Walker Atkinson***   *Psychology/Religion Pages 144*

Optimism *by Helen Keller*   **ISBN:** *1-59462-108-X*   **$15.95**
Helen Keller was blind, deaf, and mute since 19 months old, yet famously learned how to overcome these handicaps, communicate with the world, and spread her lectures promoting optimism. An inspiring read for everyone...   Biographies/Inspirational Pages 84

Sara Crewe *by Frances Burnett*   **ISBN:** *1-59462-360-0*   **$9.45**
In the first place, Miss Minchin lived in London. Her home was a large, dull, tall one, in a large, dull square, where all the houses were alike, and all the sparrows were alike, and where all the door-knockers made the same heavy sound...   Childrens/Classic Pages 88

The Autobiography of Benjamin Franklin *by Benjamin Franklin*   **ISBN:** *1-59462-135-7*   **$24.95**
The Autobiography of Benjamin Franklin has probably been more extensively read than any other American historical work, and no other book of its kind has had such ups and downs of fortune. Franklin lived for many years in England, where he was agent...   Biographies/History Pages 332

Name	
Email	
Telephone	
Address	
City, State ZIP	

☐ **Credit Card**   ☐ **Check / Money Order**

Credit Card Number	
Expiration Date	
Signature	

Please Mail to: Book Jungle
PO Box 2226
Champaign, IL 61825
or Fax to: 630-214-0564

ORDERING INFORMATION
web: *www.bookjungle.com*
email: *sales@bookjungle.com*
fax: *630-214-0564*
mail: *Book Jungle PO Box 2226 Champaign, IL 61825*
or PayPal *to sales@bookjungle.com*

Please contact us for bulk discounts

DIRECT-ORDER TERMS

**20% Discount if You Order
Two or More Books**
Free Domestic Shipping!
Accepted: Master Card, Visa,
Discover, American Express